Stay Outta Harm's Way 2: The Story of Dinah

Shiphrah Israel

TABLE OF CONTENTS

Author's Note v

Chapter One: Tim-Prison And Decisions 1

Chapter Two: Rachel-Bittersweet Hellhole 7

Chapter Three: Dinah- Recovering 12

Chapter Four: Xavier- A New Step 19

Chapter Five: Rachel-First Day Out. 22

Chapter Six: Name Ring Bells 28

Chapter Seven: Aunt Shayna Views 30

Chapter Eight: Can I See You, again? 34

Chapter Nine: Xavier-Services Denied 38

Chapter Ten: Rachel's In A Rut 41

Chapter Eleven: Dinah And Desire 46

Chapter Twelve: The Turn Up 52

Chapter Thirteen: An Ordered Hit 67

Chapter Fourteen: An Emotional Call 70

Chapter Fifteen: Jermaine And The Crew 77

Chapter Sixteen: Cruze's Mission 80

Chapter Seventeen: Don't Be Reprobate 85

Chapter Eighteen: Word On That Hit 90

Chapter Nineteen: The Rise Of Tiffany 93

Chapter Twenty: Hard To Come By. 100

Chapter Twenty-One: Rachel's Night Out. 103

Chapter Twenty-Two: Too Caught Up 109

Chapter Twenty-Three: Too Much 114

Chapter Twenty-Four: High School Memories 117

Chapter Twenty-Five: Old Communications 122

Chapter Twenty-Six: Guess Who's Back 124

Chapter Twenty-Seven: Night Gone Wrong. 132

Chapter Twenty-Eight: Kohl And Lonnie 140

Chapter Twenty-Nine: We're Having Company. 149

Chapter Thirty: The House Of James 155

Chapter Thirty-One: Prince Charming 159

Chapter Thirty-Two: Physical Therapy 167

Chapter Thirty-Three: Tiffany Is Back 174

Chapter Thirty-Four: Locked And Loaded 181

Chapter Thirty-Five: Furious 187

Chapter Thirty-Six: Character Collision 190

Cast Your Vote! 195

Discussion Questions 196

AUTHOR'S NOTE

This novel is a work of fiction. Any reference to real people, events, establishments or locales are intended only to give the fiction a sense of reality and authenticity. Other names, characters and incidents occurring in the work are either a product of the author's imagination or used in a fiction like matter. Any character that happens to share the name who is in acquaintance of the author, past or present, is purely coincidental and is no way intended to be an actual account involving the person.

Chapter One

TIM-PRISON AND DECISIONS

———⌘———

Tim slouched back in the hard-backed folding chair as he
watched Xavier approach the visitor booth he'd been
assigned. The gray concrete walls that made up the visiting
area were scuffed and dirty. The plexiglass separating pris-
oners from visitors was scratched and smudged with finger
prints. In a few places there were large cracks and divots in
the plexiglass as though an inmate had slammed the phone
headset into it. Tim ignored all of that as he watched Xavier
approach.

Pulling at the stubble on his chin, he noticed a new swag
in Xavier's step he didn't like. Were those new kicks? Here
he was looking rough in a stained orange jumpsuit, needing a
trim and overdue on a haircut. In comes this nigga that used
to run his errands looking fresh. When Xavier sat down, they
both picked up a phone handset. Tim didn't bother greeting

Xavier. He jumped straight to the point.

"I need you to put some money on my commissary," Tim said from behind the glass.

Xavier shook his head. "Damn, hello to you too. Can't even say my name before you start askin' for shit?"

Tim waved a hand dismissively, "Nigga please. No time for..."

Xavier cut him off with a quick laugh and took a long slow look around the room. "Seems to me, one thing you got is time." Looking back at Tim he said, "Anyhow, just came to see how you were doing. I ain't doing that other stuff no more."

Tim leaned forward in the chair and gripped the handset tighter. "What the hell you mean you not doing it no more? You been doing it for a whole year, now you come talkin' out the side of your neck."

"Took me a whole year to realize that you don't run me no more. This ain't the streets. I'm standing up for myself. I'm not about let no convict in an

orange jumpsuit pump fear in me."

Tim narrowed his eyes and leaned in until his nose touched the glass between them. "Yeah negro? You real tough on the other side of that glass." He cocked his fingers like a gun and pointed them in Xavier's direction. "Don't get too smart for your own good. If you not here to pay respect why you come?"

Xavier's voice took on a serious tone. "I just wanna know why man? Why you kidnap Dinah and have her prostituting for you? You knew how I felt about her."

"You knew how I felt about her," Tim said mockingly in a high-pitched tone. "You don' turned into a wimp for a whore." Leaning back in his chair he said, "Get the hell outta here with that noise over a whore."

"She's not a whore, you tried to make her out to be one. Kinda why you're here yo." Now, Xavier leaned in close, flexing on the glass between them. Visitors on either side of him side-eyed in their direction. He sighed and leaned back. Swinging a hand in Tim's direction he said, "Forget it. You ain't worth the trouble."

"Look ain't nobody about to get over on me and think they don't have to pay," Tim spat.

Xavier shook it off and stood up. "I guess that one year haven't done nothing for you yet huh. Well I hope your ass soak up every year that you got." He hung up the phone and walked away.

"Yo Xavier... X. You just gonna leave me hanging." Tim said as if Xavier could hear him from behind the glass.

***

Tim paced the length of his cell considering his options.

Money in prison brought power and control, on top of making a bad situation a little more tolerable. If you could throw a brother a few things, a magazine, stamps or even snacks they'd do your bidding. He was practically Diddy on his cell block and he meant to keep it that way. Mumbling to himself he said, "I know this negro didn't come up here and try to play me. That couldn't be what just happened," he said, punching his right fist into the palm of his left hand.

Jeffro, his cellmate, had been flipping through a magazine, relaxing in the top bunk, when Tim had come back to the cell. He looked up at the sound of Tim pacing. "What's up, what's the problem?" He swung his legs over the side and jumped down. "You good?"

Even though Tim was no longer on the streets, he'd made a name for himself during the year he'd spent on this cell block. He was well respected and people checked with him first. Tim could throw down if he had too. He'd used a mop bucket to beat the brakes off two idiots who tried to double team him in the laundry when he first arrived. His reward was two weeks in solitary confinement. A badge that meant, mess with me and there are consequences. These days, he didn't have to flex on his own. He had a crew 'round here just like back at home. And it took more than muscle to maintain a prison crew. It took funds.

The more he thought about what Xavier had just pulled,

the angrier he got. He stopped pacing and turned to face Jeffro, "This clown who use to be a part of my operations just came up here trying to be tough tony. Man, I couldn't believe I was considering his ass to be the one to take over the streets once I was ready to settle down."

"Tim look, if you need to me to handle that, I got you. You know my guys would be on it without a shadow of a doubt, just let me know what you want done."

Tim considered the offer. Having Xavier taken care of wouldn't get new money on his books but it would protect his rep in the streets and in this joint. Word travels fast both ways. He can't let people play him on the outside. That could have dangerous repercussions on the inside. "Yeah, Yeah. I hear you. Let me map some things out first, I might just take you up on that offer." After getting five years knocked off his sentence, leaving his bid at 25 years, he had to make sure things was done decently and in order.

Tim's cellmate Jeffro had been in the streets since he was ten years old. He was doing the same thing Tim was doing out in the streets. Hailing from the Rockwell projects, just a little over two hours away from Glenview, all he knew was fast money, drugs, weapons, women, break ins and drive bys. He got caught up in it all and due to his ruthless attitude and rowdy behavior he made a name for himself. The little guys that he had under him had the same ruthless and rowdy ways and when Jeffro got locked up for twelve years on gun charges and packing and transporting illegal drugs they vowed to follow in his footsteps and do as he say even from behind bars.

Chapter Two

RACHEL-BITTERSWEET HELLHOLE

W e were sitting around one of the round metal tables in the recreation area. Janice, my bunkmate, and two other women I'd become friendly with since arriving, Maria and Sheila. Maria, a tall Hispanic with a thick accent, was braiding Janice's hair into cornrows. Sheila, who was short, round and dark skinned, was flipping through photographs of her children she'd recently received in the mail. Her chubby cheeks were pushed up in a smile, but her eyes were watery. My back against the wall, I turned away from her and gazed outside on the empty yard. Soon, very soon, all of this would be nothing more than a bad dream. Absent mindedly, I toyed with a cornrow that was unraveling behind my left ear, remembering the sequence of events that had landed me here.

I'm not sure I would have changed much. Don't feel like

I had many options at the time. My so-called mother always in my face looking for dollars. Me shifting from job to job, and not for lack of trying either. It seemed like all I'd had was bad luck piled on top of worse luck. In my same position, who wouldn't have jumped into Tim's car that night? Walking the neighborhood alone trying to drown my sorrows in a cheap bottle of Moscato when a handsome looking man in a nice car rolls up trying to offer what at the time I thought was better. All I had to go home to was bills, an empty fridge and my mother with her hand out. So hell yeah, I hopped in his ride and never looked back. I was so caught up in my head that Maria had to call my name twice.

"Chica... 'ello!" María said.

"Huh?"

"Gurl where your head at? Was askin' if you want me to fix those few braids you messin' with when I'm done?"

I blinked as if I'd been dreaming and looked up to see them all staring at me. Slightly embarrassed I said, "Nah, I'm good. Prolly wash it in the shower in the morning anyway."

"I know that's right!" Janice starts popping her fingers and doing the Cabbage Patch while sitting. "Oh yeah. Oh yeah. Ra-ra goin' home soon. Ra-ra goin' home soon."

We all laughed. I didn't like Janice's nickname for me, but at least it felt like friendship. Made this private little hell I landed myself in a bit more bearable. I was going to be getting out any day now. I had been in the Lawrence County Correctional Facility for exactly 353 days. In that time, I've had to defend myself, keep my sanity and choke down an endless string of thick cut sandwiches. On my life, I will never eat thick cut meat on white bread again after I get out of here.

Janice chimed in. "Gurl wish it was me. These two years is grinding by much too slow. Sucka ass friends stopped coming to visit a couple of months into my stretch. I guess everyone's Obama phone broke 'cuz they stopped calling too."

"Fake peeps be that way," Maria said while yanking Janice's head back into place while continuing to braid her hair. "Family is all that matters. Mine keep my back whatever and wherever."

"Amen," Sheila added. "Knowing my kids is good keeps me from going beast in here."

Janice and I both laughed. That wasn't our experience with family, or friends, for that matter. "Must be nice," I said. "Mine ain't nothing like that. And the guy I was rolling with is what landed me in here."

Sheila started another long story about her family and kids. The others joined in. I tuned them all out. I didn't come from that and don't have anything like that waiting for me on the outside. I'm back at ground zero, except worse. Don't know where I'm going to lay my head when I get sprung.

And now, I have a criminal record employers can use as an excuse not to hire me. "Great," I mumbled to myself.

I'mma have to buck up, take a deep breath and figure shit out. Like when the judge handed out my sentence as a co-conspirator with Tim and gave me twelve months. It was like someone had shot me my chest. The explosion spread throughout my body. It pounded in my ears, hammered in my head and buckled my knees, but I didn't go down. I dropped my head trying not to cry or show my fear. I clamped my hands together to stop them from shaking. Until that point I'd been a bit bold and sassy with the judge. Then she dropped the hammer and reality set in. The consequence of having done nothing to help someone who I had considered my friend, Dinah, was losing my freedom as she had. Damn, karma is nothing to play with.

When I looked up again, Maria was finished braiding Janice's hair. The three of them were huddled together over a three-month-old torn up magazine. I was with them, but not. A part of their circle, but not. I was the sidekick chick. Not from their world of perpetual short stays in county or prison. I was grateful they'd accepted me which was Janice's doings. But I didn't want to make this my norm. Even though I don't regret the things I did to get money when I had to, next time I had to find a better way.

The only letters I'd received since being incarcerated

were from Dinah and my uncles. Not sure why she's still riding with me but glad that she is. She's encouraging me to find a new perspective when I exit this nightmare. Forget about being caught up with the smooth talking, new car riding, Benjamin flashing men I've known and coveted. Get mine on my own and make a fresh start. I don't need her to tell me that though. It's what I want for myself.

I hear what she's saying, but when you come from a broken childhood, sometimes you make excuses for your grind and games. You justify the evil you allow into your life. Not going to back slide or make excuses in the future. Having a person like Dinah in my life will keep me on my toes. Pushing away my self-doubt that I can live up to those expectations, I whisper to myself, "You can do it!"

Leaving me alone with the chaos running through my head, the others have gotten up from the table and drifted off in different directions. I'm alone again and on my own. Like I have been most of my life. But forget letting that define me. "I'm getting into school and find a job. Any legal job that will take me, I promised myself. Forget coming back to this hell hole.

Chapter Three

DINAH- RECOVERING

———∞∞∞———

My new bedroom is spacious with a private bathroom. We painted the walls my favorite shade of pale gray. The curtains, bedspread, and other accents are lavender. Together it's a soothing effect which was intentional. I spend long hours at my desk situated in front of a double pane window. I watch people come and go. I'm mesmerized by how the leaves dance on branches when a breeze sweeps through the trees that line our street. Here, I'm safe and isolated.

I know that I'm wounded. I'm like a kicked puppy keeping to the edge of the room and hiding in corners. Sadness stares back in me when I look in the mirror. I turn away when I catch glimpses of myself naked. Tears sting my eyes. I don't want to be this person. I want back what Tim stole from me, but I'm not sure how to get it. For my family, I wear a face of calm and slap on my "I got this," heels. I'm broken. When I'm alone, curled up on my bed tears sting my eyes as I ask myself, "Why me?"

Was I perfect? No, I wasn't. I had my skeletons like anyone else, but I was -- am, I think, a decent person. I never knowingly hurt anyone. I was trying to be on my game and do my thing. So why? Why me? Even as I ask the question, I know the answer. I paid for my brother's sins. A man chose to use me as a weapon to get even with him. Well, it worked. It hurt him, me -- my whole family. We're all recovering, but I'm the one wearing the scars. I'm the one dipped in war paint. Not them. I inhale and exhale as the tears well in my eyes. Inhale, exhale and push down the dread welling in the pit of my stomach.

There's a soft knock on my door. Ugh, I want to pretend I'm asleep but my mother would just pop her head in to check. "It's open," I said as I swiveled the chair toward the door.

"I'm heading to the store for a few things want to come? I won't take long. I just need a few things for dinner."

"Don't think so, but thanks." I painted a smile on my face, but she's not fooled.

She crossed the room and sat on the edge of the bed. "You need to start getting back to yourself again D. The new semester is only a few weeks away. What then?"

"I'm good," I fronted. "It's not that. I'm tired and have a headache."

She gives me her I know when you're lying look but doesn't push the issue. "Tomorrow then. I'm going to check out that new mall. I'm sure you need a few things." She smiles and winks. "Let's shop for some new clothes and shoes!"

At that, we both laugh. Designer shoes are one of my mother's weaknesses. A fact she and my dad often argue over. But he has his vices too, like the crazy expensive strong drink he likes to sip and drink on every night. Because she sees me smile she relents and leaves to run her errands. Now that the house is empty, I go downstairs to raid the fridge.

The kitchen to me is like something straight out of home improvement or design magazine. The appliances are stainless steel. The cabinets are off white with speckled gray and white granite countertops. A bedroom with a private bathroom was the gift for me. This kitchen is my mother's compensation for quitting her job as a social worker at one of the top middle schools in the city, to babysit me. Of course, they're not calling it that. My dad said she quit to watch over all of us better. Lies. My mother loved her job. She'd worked her way up from an assistant a few years ago. She was on her game there and she took her craft seriously. Exactly what I was working toward when... I forced the thought away. Not going to ruin the moment of feeling relaxed in my skin walking around the house without eyes on me worrying.

We've only been in the house a few months now. My dad moved us to Pearl Springs. Beautiful neighborhood with beaches, malls, restaurants, attractions and so much more. I know it was his idea for mom to stop working. He said it was so that we could spend more time together. But I know it was so she could keep a sure watch over me. It's all good most days. I like to chill in my bedroom, and she likes to cook, clean and when she has accomplished her motherly and wifely duties she would reward herself by shopping. After years of working, she might enjoy not having to punch a clock, but she's not one to be idle either.

A house like this without my mom also working was only possible because the judge granted me 20,000 dollars as punitive damages during Tim's trial. Thanks to another 20,000 from what my dad and brother took from Tim's safe, we had a nest egg of 40,000 dollars to our name. We used some of it to put down on this lovely brick home, rent to own. Simeon and I dropped money on two 2017 Toyota Camrys. My dad invested money into one of his corporate buddies' business, so every time the company made money, he made money too. Simeon picked up dad's trade and started driving trucks locally. Even though we had a nice chunk of money, Simeon knew he still had to work; daddy didn't play that.

When the new semester finally arrived, my dad had gotten iffy about me going back to school. He said he had to think about it and suggested I try going to school online first. Missing out on my last semester of college and graduating on time still had me upset. On the one hand, I wasn't sure I was ready for lots of people and whatnot. On the other, it bothered me to be handled like a child. I meant to beat this and get my life back on track. I just needed to do it at my pace and on my own terms. He eventually relented seeing how important it was to me. I think mom also reminded him at some point I had to get out there on my own and college was a safe setting to begin that process.

For now, I was playing along to get along. I didn't have the energy for arguing and drama. I don't fully feel up to the task of life on my own but I want to take the baby steps toward reclaiming what had been stolen from me. And graduating was at the top of that list.

A couple of days before the start of the semester, I was on the expressway and headed to the mall when I got this mysterious call.

"Hello, is this Dinah?" A man's voice asked.

"Yeah, who is this," I said with a cracked voice. Ever since Tim got locked up, I've been in fear that I may get a threat call or something like that.

"This Xavier, how you been doing?"

One of the guys from Glenview I remembered. "What

Shiphrah Israel

do you want with me and how did you get my new number?"

"Why you gotta be so hostile, I can't get a hey or a hel-lo?"

"Look, I don't want nothing to do with anybody that was working or dealing with Tim," I said before hanging up the phone. I marked the caller ID with his name so I'd know it was him if he tried calling again.

I continued on my way to the mall to get a couple of dresses and accessories for this beautiful weather. It's been a few months since I had officially got over that traumatic defiling situation. The first stop was Judith's Boutique. They had all the things a girl would want in her closet. Jewels, head jewelry, ointments, oils, dresses, skirts, sandals and so much more. I saw a skirt online that I really wanted and there it was right there on the rack. I picked it up and headed for the dressing room. While in the dressing room trying on this beautiful tribal print maxi skirt my phone starting ringing again.

"Hello," I answered rolling my eyes, knowing who it was.

"Dinah, could we start over?"

"Xavier, why are you playing on my phone calling me from different numbers?"

"Dinah, I haven't done nothing to you for real though. Tim is in jail. You don't have to worry about him. I just cut all ties with him. I cared about you and wanted to make sure

17

you were doing fine."

"Un huh. I'm doing okay."

"I see you moved, that's good you got away from what this broke down city has to offer."

"Yeah."

"Why you being so dull with me?"

"Because I'm trying to see what you want."

"I was wondering if I could see you some time."

"First of all, my dad or brother would never agree to that. Second of all, I live well over three and a half hours away from Glenview and Third of all, why do you want to see me?"

"I just want to see your pretty face."

"You think I'm silly. I know when a guy is running game."

"Don't think so little of me, Dinah."

"Xavier you're in that kind of lifestyle that I just can't be rolling with. I'm trying to stay out of trouble."

"Look, Dinah, I left a lot of that alone and the rest I would leave alone for you, for real."

"Nah, don't do nothing for me, do it for yourself. Thanks for checking up on me, I gotta go," I ended the conversation. I didn't know what that was about, but I can't let Xavier or anyone else get me sidetracked. I'm staying on my plan to take back what was stolen from me. This time, I'd be even better. Work even harder.

Chapter Four

Xavier- A New Step

Y'all see how Dinah just tried to play me though? I mean I understand why she felt that way. I can only imagine what she had to go through. That's the main reason why I checked Tim. I had to cut that Negro off. At the end of the day, he knew how I got down. Aint no man 'bout to play puppet master over me. Tim knew how I rolled and that's why I was next in line to run his operations.

I'm not to be played with. I gotta whole new pep in my step. Making my own money and not having to give Tim a damn dime was going good for me. Him doing what he did to Dinah, was like somebody hurt my family. She offered to help me get back on track and ole girl believed in me when nobody else did, even my buddies laughed at me when I told them I was trying to get back in school. But she didn't and because of that, I'm riding with her whether she knows it or not. I'll eventually get through to her.

I just been out here making money. Tim being in prison equaled more money for me. I recently took over my mom's crib. I had put her in rehab, so she could get herself together. I couldn't keep seeing my OG struggle like that. Other than that, I just been kicking it with the guys and making money the best way I know how. With nobody playing overseer over me; I've been getting my name out here in the streets as well as my product. This allowed me to get things that I wanted.

But, I felt like I was missing something and that was Dinah. Now, trust me, I know how the men in her family get down, but I'm willing to fight in the field for her. I know I'm young, twenty-three to be exact, but one thing my pops taught me was that if you have a gut feeling about something, you gotta listen to it and go for it.

My guys may laugh at me, but not for long. They know I never been the type to care what anybody gotta say. Even though I was out here hustling, I still had to at least get some education under my belt. I needed Dinah's help but most importantly I needed her in my life.

I'll just shoot her a text or something, because she not about to keep hanging up on me. Anyways, I was riding around in my new 2017 Hyundai Sonata... Nah, let me stop playing with y'all, it was a rental that I had to give back in a couple of days. I had to role to Havenport to handle some business. I know I told Dinah I would leave this life alone, but I had to make some ends meet. I had to make some things happen, especially if I was trying to get next to her.

"Domo," I said to one of my clients as I pulled up.

"Xavier, please tell me you got that package for me?"

"You think I'll ride to Havenport if I didn't," I laughed as we did our exchange. That was 5,000 dollars easy.

"You know I had to lay low with this work you wanted."

"Ah ha, well you got yours and I got mines." Domo said while giving each other dap.

"Domo you a fool, hit me up, if you need anything else." I said before pulling off.

Like I said, I've been having to lay low with my product. Even though my name was out there. It's a small circle that I worked with. If you heard about my product and wanted something, you had to get it from somebody in my circle. I couldn't just be pulling up on everybody. I was low key like Ace from Paid in Full. Just like he made it out, I am too. In a while this will soon just be something to look back on.

Chapter Five

RACHEL-FIRST DAY OUT.

"Rachel Davis, today must be your lucky day. Release day for you," The female guard said as she approached her cell. Rachel grabbed all her belongings and letters she received over a twelve-month span.

"Oh my Gosh, thank you. These twelve months have felt like forever," Rachel expressed.

"Let me tell you something," The female officer grabbed Rachel by the collar. "I don't want to ever see you in here again. Do you understand me? You, what--twenty-two years old. You seem like a decent girl, but I can tell you simple, you just simple, girl. I really hoped you learned your lesson in here. Learn how to say no, don't just be out here doing anything and please don't let another man get in your head, ya hear. I hope you remember those three things, if nothing else," The guard was nothing but serious with Rachel.

"Yes ma'am, I understand."

"You better or your ass will be right back in here."

"I said I understand. I got you."

"I just gotta give it to you straight, now go return that DOC jumpsuit and let's go get your belongings and discharge papers, you got two people waiting on you."

Walking through the county with the guard felt like she was walking into freedom again. She couldn't help but reminisce on walking the opposite way of the same hall through the county when she first started her sentence exactly one year ago. Shaking that thought off, she just wanted to step foot outside.

While Rachel got her discharge papers. Her two uncles were waiting for her.

"Look at my niece, come here girl," Said her Uncle Tony alongside his brother Uncle David. He hugged her tight and rubbed the top of her cornrows as if she was a long-lost puppy.

"Hey, Uncle Tony and Uncle David," Rachel received their hugs and greetings.

"The question is, how are you?"

"I'm just happy to be out."

"That's what I wanna hear." Uncle Tony expressed.

They walked out of the Lawrence County Correctional Facility and headed towards the car. It was about 85 degrees outside with a nice breeze. "What a good day to get out," Rachel said as she smelled the summer air. "I know you hungry, so me and Uncle David here are gonna take you out to eat." Uncle Tony started up the car.

Lawrence county, Metro county, Glenview, Rockwell, Havenport. Where y'all at? It's 85 degrees in the city and I know the ladies looking pretty. Get out and enjoy this whether as we play the latest hit from rap sensation...Montae X. The Radio personality sounded through the speakers as Uncle David cut the radio up. Rachel rolled her eyes. Hearing the name Montae X, grinded her gears.

"Maybe tomorrow, your Aunt Shayna can take you to go get your hair, nails and feet did and whatever else it is that you females like to do."

Rachel stared out the window watching young girls play jump rope, kids ride their bikes and people going in and out of shopping centers. Seeing that made her smile. It was the little things that made her feel like she had to get it together.

"How that sound?" Uncle Tony asked again.

"Huh?"

"I said, my wife Shayna can take you to go get your hair, nails and feet done tomorrow."

"Aww, that sounds good. I'm just grateful that y'all taking me back in."

"That's what family is for. We got you."

"Speaking of family, how's my momma doing?"

"Same ole, same ole. You know how our sister Veronica is. She been looking for handouts, but I told her she gotta get herself together first. Ain't nothing wrong with her," Uncle David responded. The sound of his voice became irritated even speaking of his sister.

"Yep, if she's is able-bodied, that means she can get a job," Uncle Tony agreed.

"She didn't call you?" Both Uncle Tony and Uncle David asked Rachel wanting to know.

"I can count on my hand how many times my mom called me. She claimed she was going to come to visit me if she got a ride," Rachel looked out the car window.

"Aww hell, Veronica is full of crap. I'm through with the excuses she like to make," Uncle David snapped.

"She could have called any one of us, but she didn't. That's okay though, you know how your mom is, it shouldn't even be a surprise. We all saw how she turned out when you were fourteen years old. I honestly blame all of this on her. If she would have kept her head on straight, you would have not been in the predicaments that you had to be in, but I'm not going to beat a dead horse. Are y'all ready to eat?" Uncle Tony asked changing the subject as they pulled up to Morgan Buffet and Grille.

"I am." Rachel hopped out the backseat.

"I bet you are, my eldest niece. I know about them jail sandwiches and slop they like to give inmates." Uncle Tony said putting his arm around her shoulder walking towards the restaurant.

Once they paid and got seated. They headed straight to the buffet. Rachel sniffed the aroma of the foods they had on display before grabbing a plate. She piled her plate with barbeque beef brisket, mash potatoes, corn on the cob and cornbread muffins. She was aiming for food that could resemble a home-cooked meal.

"Now Rachel, we know you been in jail for twelve months and we know you don't have much. So, in addition to taking you in, me and your Uncle David here wanna give you four hundred dollars to help you get back on your feet."

"Yeah, we need you to use that money for things that you need. You know, like getting new clothes, shoes, your hair did and other little personals. I don't wanna hear that you were out here selling yourself short." Uncle David told her.

"Thank y'all so much and you don't have to worry about that Uncle David."

"Rachel don't let being locked up hinder you. You hear? You are young and there are still opportunities out there for you."

"I will take that into consideration Uncle Tony, thanks."

"That's all that matter."

After eating at the buffet and Rachel's uncles giving her a lecture. They were on their way to Uncle Tony's house with his wife Shayna whom she was going to be staying with.

Chapter Six

NAME RING BELLS

Jeffro was drawing a picture of his mother, thanks to Tim sharing his commissary, he was able to get some drawing materials. "Have you thought about how ole' boy came up here and tried to play you?" Jeffro asked. Even being in prison couldn't stop his ruthless ways.

"I'm glad you brought that up," Tim rose up off his bed. "All I've done for his ass and he turn around and talk crazy to me over a female. Well, just like she had to pay, he gotta pay," Tim said getting amped up.

"That's what I'm talking about bro, I can handle that for you, for real though."

"Yeah? Hold on though, I don't know yo guys."

"You know me though, that's all that matter. Unless you already got somebody to handle it for you?"

"Nawl, my other little guys Jermaine, Kenny, Rodney

and Cruze wouldn't do it."

"Man, they mad disrespectful if they don't follow their leader. I see it like this, even though you behind bars, you gotta keep your name ringing in the streets."

"Nawl, it aint that. It's just I told them to never turn on each other no matter what."

"Un huh, they listen to that though, huh? Well look, my guys are just like me. I tell them what to do and they follow orders. If one detail is done differently they already know what could happen to them. I'll have somebody trailing their asses next."

"You sure about this huh?" Tim looked at Jeffro.

"Bro, you think this the first time I sent out orders from in here? I told you my name still ring bells from this jail cell."

"Okay, well let's do it then."

"That's what I wanna hear." Jeffro said as they gave each other a pound. "Just tell me what you want done and it's done."

Jeffro was serious. He and Tim was tight. They shared their commissary with each other, put each other up on knowledge and on their cell block, if anybody had a problem with Jeffro then they had a problem Tim and if anybody had a problem with Tim then they had a problem with Jeffro, so this situation was no different.

Chapter Seven

AUNT SHAYNA VIEWS

"I've been meaning to get you to myself. Now that your uncle and cousin are gone, we can talk." Aunt Shayna sipped her hazelnut coffee. Rachel shot her a side look, not knowing what to expect out of this conversation.

"First off, you can be plain ole Rachel when you around me. I don't do the two-faced thing, hiding who you really are." Shayna flipped through the channels of the kitchen tv. "Now, I know a little bit about why you were in jail, but that's none of my business. However you make money is how you make it, honey. Your momma didn't give a damn about what was going on with you, so aye, you took it upon yourself to obtain the necessary things to survive, right?"

"Right, I had to do what I had to do." Rachel opened up.

"This, I know, niece. You ain't even gotta tell me. Don't let that get you down though, Rachel. Now that we have a little free time, we can go get some mani's and pedi's and then we can go to the shop, so they can tackle that head, I noticed you got some split ends." Shayna said as she touched her hair. They both laughed.

"Okay, sounds like a plan," Rachel responded.

"Oh, and I'm also gonna get you some business attire clothes and a phone. I'm the cool auntie and you can come to me about anything, but if you're over eighteen and staying here, you gotta be bringing in something, that's why I said, however you make your money is how you make it."

"Aunt Shayna you're something else."

"I'm just stating facts my lovely niece, now let's go get ready so we can head out."

They both went upstairs to get ready. Rachel put her hair in a sheek ponytail, a blue sun dress and some coach flip flops that Aunt Shayna let her wear. After getting herself together she walked in another room where Aunt Shayna was. It was her beauty room. Shayna was thirty-four years old and still knew how to keep up. Rachel noticed Shayna's Venus floral dress, her Belma wedge heels, her diamond cut earrings and her jet-black hair that touched her back. She watched as she applied her Black Opal foundation and her lavender purple lipstick. She looked like she was about to walk down the runway for a modeling event. Rachel admired her style.

"Your uncle wants us to go get you some things, so that's what were about to do. First were gon' hit the nail shop and then we can go from there."

****

We pulled off in Aunt Shayna's Grey Chevy Equinix. She seemed cool. I haven't seen her since I was seventeen years old. I guess she felt that now I was twenty-two, we could build that bond. She seemed like a totally different person around my Uncle Tony. I didn't know if that was a good thing or a bad thing. Would me kicking it with Shayna bite me in the ass later or is she just genuinely cool and down to earth as she appears to be.

"You ready to go get some pedicures?" Shayna asked as she put her car in park.

"Yes, I am, it has been twelve months without attention to these feet." I chuckled. "Thanks again this trip is much needed."

"You're welcome. My feet need some love too."

We both walked into "Nails Supreme" waiting to be called for our pedicures. The wait wasn't that long before they called to service us. We both sat on the leather vibrating seats while soaking our feet in the soothing water. Right before the feet masseuse came over to get started on our feet, Shayna spoke.

"Rachel, like I said earlier, and I will say it again; I understand why you did what you did."

Where is she going with this?

"Truth be told, I was headed down that same road, but your Uncle Tony saved me. Made sure I didn't have to be patrolling the streets at the tender age of seventeen, to make money for the things I felt like I wanted and needed. Now, who am I to say if that path is right or wrong? You gotta know what works best for you. It's people who busted their ass for a degree and barely making it. We are living in a tough world, I'm not about to shake my finger at you. People act like they weren't young before. Like, if a smooth guy came offering them more than what they have, they wouldn't accept. Especially, if they not getting no love at home." Shayna said before telling the nail tech her color. She was making some valid points. It seemed like she's was the only one not judging me or telling me how they never wanna see go down that road again. First of all, this is my life and secondly, that was the last thing I wanted to hear. Aunt Shayna understanding me was like a breath of fresh air.

Chapter Eight

CAN I SEE YOU, AGAIN?

D inah was on her laptop finishing up some homework
for her Biology class when her phone rang.

512-714-0080 would like to face time you. Is what appeared
on her phone. She accepted the call, voice only.

"It's Xavier, connect the video."

"How I suppose to know that this was you." Dinah said
as she connected the call.

"There goes that girl," Xavier said as the video call connected. Although she didn't want to, she couldn't help but
smile.

"Did I just see a smile?"

"Oh my gosh, what do you want?" Dinah asked in a
playing manner.

"Trying to see what you been up too."

"The only thing I'm up to is getting my life back on

track and doing this homework, when did you become team iPhone?"

"I got my ways of getting what I want."

"Okay, so what do you want with me?"

I'm checking on you, trying to see how you been holding up."

"What you checking on me for, don't you have other females, you could be calling or getting with?"

"I'm not going to lie, I do have other females I could call, but I don't want too. Plus, they are not as important as you."

"Okay, so they are of some importance, but not that much? Xavier, get off my phone playing games."

"Damn, what's up with your hostility against me?"

"I'm not being hostile with you, you just calling me with foolishness. Plus, you're interrupting me in the middle of my homework assignment."

"I see you. You got on your little reading glasses, looking all educated and pretty."

"Thanks' for the compliment."

"Speaking of education, you know I need your help, right?"

"With?"

"I got this placement test coming up soon and I wanna pass."

"I don't know, Xavier."

"What is it that you don't know?"

"I just don't know if I would be wasting my time, again."

"You wasn't wasting your time the first time. I soaked up all that knowledge you taught me."

"Can't tell, don't look like you using it."

"You know, I got better in math because of you."

"Right, using that skill to count how much money you making on the streets and how much product you can flip."

"It aint even like that and what you know about flipping products."

"I'm not slow and I am from the gritty streets of Glenview."

"Un huh, the gritty streets, huh?"

"Dinah?" She heard her brother Simeon's voice and steps approaching her room.

"Gotta go Xavier, bye," Dinah rushed off the phone ending the video chat before her brother could see who it was.

Standing in the doorway of her room, Simeon asked. "Who you were just on face time with?"

"A friend."

"A friend, huh? I saw male features."

"Simeon can you just let up, I'm not simple and what are you in my room anyways?"

"Dinah, now why would I let up?" Simeon said as he sat in her computer chair.

"Because you and dad should trust me enough to know that I will never make a stupid mistake again."

"Is that right?"

"Aint that's what I said."

"Don't be getting smart with me and for the record I will never let up. You my little sister and I care about you. I may have a funny way of showing it, but the love is there. You got that?"

"Un huh, I hear you."

"Now, if I got anything to do with it, I'm going to stay hard on you. I'm gonna wanna know what you doing, what you getting into, who you with, where you going, and who you on face time with." He emphasized.

"But, I'm trying to tell you, you don't have to do that."

"I know I don't have to, but I'm going to."

"Okay, big bro, whatever you say."

"Now, I'm about to head out to work. I'm stopping by that soul food joint "Southern house Kitchen that just opened up when I get off work, you want something?"

"Just call me whenever you get there, so you can tell me what they got."

"Alright, lil sis. Love ya." He gave her a kiss on the forehead before exiting her room.

Chapter Nine

XAVIER-SERVICES DENIED

―――⊶∞⊷―――

"Bro, pass the bottle." Rodney insisted Jermaine. "Man, calm down. You act like you not gon' get no Henny."

"How about both of y'all calm down, because last time I checked, me and Cruze are the only ones who put money down on this bottle of strong drink." I took a sip from my cup.

"That's because y'all the only two out there working hard," Rodney responded.

"You out here putting out the same work we putting out. You just making an excuse to keep your ends in your pockets, that's what that is." We all laughed.

"Man, I still can't believe Tim's ass. What was he thinking?" Rodney shook his head, switching the subject.

"I'm saying, we supposed to be his guys, he aint even let

us know he was running a business like that," Kenny added

"His ass slow, that's what he is. I confronted his ass not too long ago about that." I said in an angry tone.

"Aint you the one who put money on his commissary though?" Kenny asked.

"Look, services denied. I had to realize his ass don't run me."

"Wait, I'm still on the first part you said. What you mean you confronted Big Tim?" Rodney asked.

"What you mean, what I mean? I went up there and told him he was petty as hell for doing some dumb shit like that. What can he do to me? His ass locked up." I said slightly amped up.

"All over that girl?" Kenny responded.

"And, nigga. What you mean, all over that girl?"

"Bro, I'm just saying she ain't even let you in and you head over heels for her."

"Kenny shut the hell up for real, before I really take it there with yo ass. You sitting here drinking my liquor, meanwhile yo ass don't know what you're talking about and she's not just some girl," I snapped. The guys started laughing seeing how serious I was over the whole situation.

"Bro, all I'm saying is, I would have never thought you will be damn near in love." He still joked.

"Just mind your damn business. That's what you can do."

I grabbed a slice of pizza off the table.

"Aye Kenny, leave my bro Xavier alone," Jermaine chimed in. "I see it like this. Tim did what he did, he's in jail, he gotta suffer the consequences. I still got my lil customers in the streets and guess what? All that money comes back to me. It aint no more pushing and moving for Tim. So, Kenny if you take it as a lost, so be it, but I take it as a gain." Jermaine said taking the words right outta my mouth.

"Cruze, what you gotta say man. You always get real quiet when you on that damn phone." Jermaine laughed.

"All of y'all crazy, but on another note this girl just hit me up talking about she throwing a party and talk around town is everybody that's somebody supposed to be there. Y'all tryna go?" Cruze asked.

"Where it's gonna be at." I asked.

"At "The Set" on Sunday."

"On Sunday?" Rodney asked.

"Yeah, on Sunday's they have half off on venues."

"Count me in. A party is a party. Females, drinks and potential customers." Jermaine said hyped up. "Bro let your little friend know, we will be there."

Disagreements and misunderstandings - just part of the brotherhood. It was a normal night. When we were done handling business on the streets, we hung out at Rodney's crib. We ordered a pizza, bought some drinks and chilled.

Chapter Ten

RACHEL'S IN A RUT

Time was passing, and I needed to get back into my groove. I put applications for five jobs, and I applied to Tanner Heights Vocational Community College about two week ago. Three out of the five places weren't interested in hiring me, and I was just waiting to hear back from Tanner Heights.

I slipped on my house shoes and went to check the mail. Walking through the living room towards the front door felt dreadful, I was hoping to receive good news with my name on it. When I got the mail, I noticed two letters with my name on it, the rest I put on the kitchen counter. I paced back to my room, hoping for the best. The piece of mail with the Tanner Heights logo had my heart pounding. If I get accepted into Tanner Heights, this would be one of my biggest accomplishment since graduating high school and getting a job. Here it goes, let's see what it says.

Dear, Rachel Davis

Thank you for considering Tanner Heights Vocational Community College, where the mind and Education meets. The Admissions Committee has carefully reviewed your application. I am sorry to inform you that we are unable to offer you a spot for our next semester.

Reason for Rejection: Background Charges.

Thanks for your interest in Tanner Heights.

What was I thinking? It was no way I was going to get into Tanner Heights. Tanner Heights was the top community college in the city. I was really interested in their cosmetology courses. If I would have gotten in, that would have been fast and easy money for me, without having to do anything illegal.

I threw the letter on the dresser and slouched on my bed kinda upset that I kept getting rejected. When I got up, I stared at the other piece of mail with my name on it. What could this be? When I looked at it closely, in the upper left-hand corner I saw Tim's name. I shook my head and blinked twice to make sure my mind wasn't playing tricks on me.

How in the hell did he get this address? I opened the mail with my heart racing for some strange reason, as if it was another rejection letter. The letter read

Dear, Rachel

I know you just got out. I need you to come see me ASAP.

That's all he wrote in the letter. I just sat there wondering what Tim really wanted with me. An apology would be nice, but you never know with him. I was debating in mind if I should go or not.

"Ughh, this is too much for one day." I fell onto my bed.

***

Rachel sat there waiting to be greeted by Tim from behind the glass. While running her hand through her hair, Tim was walking up to the glass when she picked up the phone.

"Tim." She said, not giving him the proper greeting.

"Rachel, how you been? You still looking good."

"Un huh."

"Damn, like what's wrong with you. Yo ass already getting on the phone upset."

"What you want me to say to you? Oh, let me guess-- Hi, Tim, how has prison been treating you?"

"Don't start with me Rachel. I'm dealing with a lot as is, but since you're asking, it's been okay, I guess. I been surviving. I got five years knocked off my sentence."

"Sounds good, looks like they're showing you mercy up in here."

"I wouldn't call it that, but I guess."

"Okay, so what's up? Why you tell me to come up here?"

"Look, everybody turning on me, you all I got right now

and before you say anything about last year's situation, I'm sorry you had to spend twelve months in the joint, if I could, I would have added that extra year to my sentence."

"What about your boys, your little guys you had working for you?"

"I mean they checked on me in the beginning, but they need somebody leading them. Without me leading them, it aint much money they can make."

"So, what makes you think, I could help you? You were leading me too," She said in a helpless tone.

"And I can still lead you sweet heart."

"Oh hell no, Tim." She shook her head. "I'm not falling into your trap again. I just can't. I came up here because I wanted to hear an apology, now you trying to propose a business deal with me, are you serious?"

"Rachel, just hear me out."

"What, Tim?" She rolled her eyes.

"Okay, I still got some contacts on me. If I put some calls in, you can put in a little work out in the streets and boom, we both will get paid."

"Tim, I don't plan on getting back into that lifestyle."

"Like I told you before, you the only one that can help me. My top lil guy on the street turned his back on me completely, but I got something for his ass, but Rachel without you, I'm dead. I need to eat in here, I need money on my books, I need to be clean up in here."

"I just don't know. I can get a job and send you in some money here and there." Rachel responded.

"That sounds cool and all, but baby ten dollars an hour can't help me. I would need that whole check just to try to keep myself up, up in here. That's why I'm trying to tell you, this business deal that I got mapped out would keep both of us making money."

"Tim, can we change the subject because I'm not trying to hear that. I just got out of jail, you think I wanna go back?"

Chapter Eleven
DINAH AND DESIRE

I was in the parking lot of the Pearl Springs mall in my car, minding my business. This is where I came to spend a lot of my alone time. Singing along to the songs that were playing on my 90's playlist set to shuffle mode and admiring my blue and silver freshly did manicure and pedicure. My phone vibrated in my purse.

"Hello," I answered not recognizing the number

"Dinahhh!" My cousin Desire squealed over the phone. I knew her voice from anywhere.

"Hey cuz, long time no hear."

"I know Dinah, I been trying to get caught up with this college stuff, girl, but I kept telling myself as soon as I got some free time I was gonna call my you. How you been?"

"I been cool, you know. Getting myself back on track."

Desire was my favorite cousin, we were only six months

apart, and we were closer than ever. She was like my other half. I hadn't talked her in a long time, but that's what happens when life just gets ahold of you. Desire and I were just alike, and we were raised exactly the same. Our fathers are brothers, and both of their households are built on the same values.

"Cuz, I heard about what happened with you last year. Man, I wanted to come to your aid so bad, when I heard about the situation. I was ready to snap, crackle and pop, but I'm glad they locked his ass up, and I'm glad you're okay."

"Yeah, I'm cool. Thank you for being concerned about me. What uncle Judah been doing?" I asked trying to change the subject.

"Girl, same ole, same ole, trying to run everything I do like I aint twenty-one years old."

"Now you know, Uncle Judah don't play." I laughed.

"Now you know, Uncle Levi don't play, why you talking." She tried to come back at me.

"Girl, whatever," I rolled my eyes as if she could see me.

"On a lighter note, do you wanna hang out with me tonight.?"

"So, you really want me to drive two hours away to Havenport?"

"Um, that's exactly what I want you to do. You know you miss me."

"Whatever and yeah, I kinda do, let me call my dad and ask and then I'll call you back to let you know."

"Yes, it's gonna be just like old times, but okay call me back to let me know what's up."

After I got off the phone with Desire. I started my car and pulled out of the parking lot. Getting a little air would be nice. Just clearing my mind and having some fun like the good ole days with my favorite cousin. I dialed my dad.

"Hey daddy."

"Hey baby, what you doing?"

"I just came from getting my nails and toes did."

"Aww okay, that's good."

"Daddy, I was wondering if I could go spend the night and hang out with Desire."

"Aww, you finally heard from your buddy, huh. That's fine. That's my niece. That's who you should have been kicking it with in the first place, instead of that fast ass girl, Rachel."

"Okay daddy, I'm about to be on my way home to get a few things and then I'm just gonna head out to her house."

"Alright, I'm out and about, so I may not see you when I get home."

"Okay, daddy. I'll see you whenever I get back then."

"Okay, love ya." He said as we ended the call.

It just wouldn't be my daddy if he didn't give me some

type of lecture. It's like he had to find something to go in about. That's all the more of why this fresh air is needed.

***

I went home packed a few clothes, shoes and make up and was headed to Desire's house. It was almost a two hour drive to Havenport, so I texted her when I was about three blocks away. When I pulled up, her thirsty self was already outside waiting for me.

I parked in front of their house and grabbed my Love Pink duffle bag. "Ahhhhhh." We both yelled and jumped up and down as we hugged each other.

"Dinah, you don't know how much I missed you," She said as we both walked into the living room.

"Hey, Uncle Judah." I went over to give him a hug.

"Heyy, my lovely niece. What brings you by?"

"You know, just spending some time with Desire, that's all."

"You know I wanted to kill that nigga that was degrading you. I'm worse than my brother Levi. I wouldn't have let his ass live to tell his story." Uncle Judah said as if I was still in the midst of the situation.

"Yeah, I'm good though."

"That's good. So, what do you girls got planned for today?"

"Well later on tonight, were just gonna probably go out to eat, catch a movie or do some sightseeing down town with a couple of my other friends." Desire responded.

"Alright, I know you two wanna catch up, so gon' head, just let me know when y'all about to leave out."

Desire and I did some catching up and by the time we poured our lives out to one another, the night was upon us. We both did our hair and put on our fits. Desire's real hair was cut into a curly bob. She put on a black skirt with a purple and black sequin top and some gladiator sandals. Me on the other hand, put on a red pleated skirt and a simple Love pink black shirt. We both looked the part.

"Girl, we look too cute, let take a picture." Desire went straight to her camera. After taking the picture, she asked, "What's your Instagram name."

"Simply_DinahIsrael, now are you ready go? I'm ready to eat."

"Okay, let's go, we gonna take your car, because I'm low on gas right now."

"Alright, so you want me to run my gas out after driving almost two hours," I playingly said.

"Look you the one who got the money, pulling up in a brand-new Toyota Camry." She laughed.

"Girl, let's just go."

"Daddy, we about to head out." Desire yelled to the other side of the hallway.

"Alright girls, have fun."

"Okay, love ya." Desire said as we went down the stairs and headed to the front door. We got in the car and I put on my 90's rnb playlist. I fixed my rearview mirror and then looked in it to make sure my lipstick was on properly.

"So, where you trying to eat at?" I asked.

"Girl, do you really think we about to go out to eat—Ughh, no. We bout to hit up this party." Desire snapped her fingers.

"What the hell you mean, we about to hit up a party?"

"Dinah, just calm down. This girl I know having a party at "The Set" and it's about to bring the whole city out. It just wouldn't be right if we didn't show up."

"Desire, I can't stand you. I still want something to eat tho, so I'm about to stop at Tony's Burger Shack.

"Okay, we can do that, but we going to this party."

I can't believe Desire just pulled this "We going to a party" thing on me, especially since we just started back hanging out.

"Girl, if Uncle Judah finds out, he's going to kill us and then he's gonna bring us back to life and then my dad is going to kill us again."

Desire laughed. "Girl, we just getting some fresh air and having a little fun, didn't you say you needed some air anyways?"

"Yeah, I did. So, where's this party at?"

Chapter Twelve

THE TURN UP

Xavier and his boys pulled up to "The Set" in Cruze's Buick Regal

"Man, this thang looking too turned up already and this just the outside of the place." Jermaine said as they pulled up to the scene. They were ready to get out the car.

"Man, is it any spaces left, this thang tight." Cruze said trying to get a good parking spot.

"There go one up there." Xavier told him.

Eagar to get out of the car, Cruze said, "Y'all ready to meet some females and make some money?"

"You know I am." Jermaine replied. Xavier, Cruze, Jermaine, Rodney and Kenny all walked towards the front entrance. The parking lot was packed with people socializing, the front entrance was packed with people socializing, so the guys could just imagine what the inside was looking like.

All the attention was on Xavier and his crew. Women were eyeing them like the hood rich and hood famous stars they were aiming to be.

The outside scene was lit, people socializing everywhere, rocking their best fits, had it looking like a high school hallway at passing period.

They made their way to the inside. They had to peep the whole scene before making a move.

"Hey Cruze." The girl hosting the party spoke. "You and your guys names are on the V.I.P list. That mean y'all get free drinks and all."

"Alright, thanks sweetie, we bout to check that out." They walked up the stairs to the VIP section like celebrities swagged head to toe singing along to Montae X's song that poured through the speakers: *I'm getting money, I'm getting money. Haters looking funny, they looking funny. Females be up on me, they be up on me. Shout out my block boys, we repping stony, we repping stony.* That song had the party turned up. The crowd sang along as they jumped up and down and rocked back and forth. The bass shooked the room, which had the females hyped and the guys doing a simple rock, lean and two-step.

"Do you guys need anything?" The bartender that was assigned to the VIP area asked.

"Yeah, let me get some Hennessey on the rocks." Cruze requested

"Let me get a shot of Cîroc Amaretto." Xavier added.

"Coming right up."

"Man, they wasn't lying when they said this party was 'bout to bring the whole city out. Just look at this." Cruze and Xavier over looked the party from the VIP's balcony. "This is just the type of love I need coming out of the joint."

"Here you go, Hennessey on the rocks for you and a shot of Amaretto Cîroc for you." The bartender came to serve.

"Look, I just got a text. I'm about to go check on some of my connects outside, so I'm about to be in the front for a minute, hang tight." Cruze announced.

****

Jermaine was out handling his business; the other guys were talking to some females and I was just laying low and pepping the scene. From up here, the VIP section was the equivalent to the Skybox at a basketball game. I took me a few more sips of Cîroc and watched as the people came in and out of the building. After about ten minutes of checking out the party, I was about to embrace this VIP action, but I noticed a familiar face. I shook my head and leaned in forward over the VIP balcony. I knew that face from anywhere. I thought it was just the Cîroc playing mind games, but I never forget features, and I could see that natural hair from a mile away.

Is that really her, Nawl, it can't be. Her people would never let her come to a party in Havenport. I know that's her tho. That's her whole swag. Natural hair, skirt, style. The whole nine. What the hell she's doing here?

"Yo, Kenny. I'll be right back. If anybody ask where I'm at. I'm on the main level." I said as I walked down the stairs.

****

"Desire, I still can't believe I let you talk me into coming to this party" Dinah swayed back and forth to a chill beat.

"Girl, you still tripping off that? You the one that said you needed to get some air."

"That's the excuse you coming with? But I suppose you're right. This party is kinda cool, even though, I usually don't come to events like this."

"See, I got you, just trust me." After that they both was just feeling the scene. Dinah felt a bit out of place, like she said, these type of events were pretty rare to her, but the party scene was enticing.

Xavier moved through the crowd, it took him about ten minutes to get to where Dinah was at. He chuckled at her dancing. She moved side to side to Prince Dub's rnb jam "Something about You," with the little rhythm she did have. In the process of getting to her, he saw a guy approach her asking if she wanted to dance, she turned him down. "*Good Girl*," Xavier said in his head. He snuck up on her and slowly put his hands over her eyes. Desire wasn't paying attention until, Dinah panicked.

"Guess who," Xavier smiled.

"Oh, hell nawl, who are you and why do you have your hands over my cousin's eyes," Desire snapped.

"Desire, who is this?" She said while trying to pull his hands off of her.

"I don't know, but I'm about to mase his ass, if he don't tell us."

"Calm down Desire, just give me a description."

"You sure Cuz?"

"Yeah, just do it." Dinah replied having an idea of who it was.

"Okay, he's dark skinned, got a little beard, about five-eleven."

"Xavier?" Dinah said as she grabbed his hands from off her eyes.

"Dinah, what the hell you doing here?"

"What are you doing here? Since you wanna ask questions like you my father."

"I'm just shocked. I would have never expected to see you, here. In Havenport, at a party. I mean, I'm glad to see you, but, really what you doing out here?"

"My cousin lives out this way."

"Hey cousin." Xavier said in a funny tone

"Hello, who are you?"

"Oh, Dinah haven't told you?"

"Um, I don't think you that important to my cousin."

"Anyways, Dinah. You can come to Havenport, but you can't come see me, huh?"

"Actually, my cousin here, tricked me into coming to this event."

"Well, thank you cousin." Xavier smiled as he looked at Desire.

"Boy, bye." Desire waved him off. "…But I'm going to let y'all two chat it up. I'm about to go speak to my home-girls. Dinah, just call me if you need me"

"Okay, I will." Dinah watched her cousin walk off before looking back at Xavier.

"You look nice."

"If that's what you want to call it." She responded.

"Let me talk to you? Let's take a walk outside." Xavier insisted as he grabbed her hand.

The outside scene had died down. People were still out there drinking and conversing, but it wasn't crowded. The breeze blew as Xavier and Dinah started their stroll around the venue.

"So, if you don't mind me asking—how you been feeling

since everything transpired?"

Before Dinah could answer, she put her head down and began walking slower. "I've been okay, just trying to get it out of my mind, you know."

"I get it, Dinah, you are upset, but don't beat your pretty self up about it." Xavier said as he stopped her in her tracks. He looked into her eyes and said. "It doesn't have to be all bad. You can get through this. I can help you get through this."

She tried to ignore his sentimental moment as they continued to walk. "Thanks, but no thanks."

"See, that's the problem. You keep telling yourself that you don't need help, that you can do this shit on your own, but you can't."

"I'm just saying, I don't want to keep thinking about it, but it just pops up. It tries to take hold of me. It tries to stop me from reaching my goals, my plans and the things I got set for myself."

"Well, let me be the first to say, I'm sorry Dinah. When I found out the truth about what was going on. I felt like somebody was hurting my family. I mean I stop talking to Ti—I'm not even gonna say his name, but I set him straight about what he did to you. It was no way I was gonna continue working for him after what he pulled."

"Thank you, but I already told you, you don't have to do

nothing for me or because of me."

"Look." He stopped walking, again. "Look at me. This is not something I did just to do. That was serious, and I don't play when it comes to people I care about."

"Okay, my bad." She said seeing that he wasn't taking this matter lightly.

"How your folks been taking it? If you don't mind me asking."

"My dad went crazy if that's what you want to know, but they been taking well for now, just been trying to keep me sheltered and not wanting me to be out too long. The whole situation just shifted everything." Dinah let out a sigh.

"You don't look so well talking about it. I gotta get you back in good vibes. You wanna go grab a bite to eat? It's a diner about half a mile up."

"Ummm, I don't know about that one." She gritted her teeth.

"I can grab my buddy Cruze's keys and we can go."

"Nawl, my car is right around this corner."

"So, is that a yes?"

"I suppose."

They waked to Dinah's car, before starting her car she texted Desire to let her know she was going for a quick spin. "So, where's this diner?"

"When you pull out of this lot, you're gonna make a left

and just keep straight for four and a half blocks."

Although four and a half blocks were only about three minutes. Awkwardness was in the air as they both got in the car together.

She rode the four blocks before saying. "Is that it?" Breaking the silence.

"Yep, there it is." Xavier responded as Dinah put on her turning signal.

"Table for two?" The waiter asked as she grabbed two menus.

"Yes."

"Okay, follow me… Is a booth okay?"

"That's fine," Xavier took the lead.

Xavier made sure Dinah sat down comfortable before sitting across from her. Five minutes later, the waiter came back ready to take their orders.

"So, I'll take y'alls breakfast sampler. Strawberry and crème on the pancakes, American cheese on the eggs and turkey bacon."

"Got it and for you sir?"

"I'll take the Double Granados burger and cheese fries, light on the mayo."

"Okay and for you drink, sir?"

"I'll take a fruit punch."

"Ma'am?"

"I'll take a Raspberry lemonade."

"Okay, I'll put these orders in and drinks will be coming right up."

"Breakfast at night, huh? What an appetite."

"It's just what I got a taste for. So, what you wanted to talk about here, that we couldn't talk about at the party?"

"I could have talked to you there, but it's better to talk it over with food."

"Well you got me alone, so what's up?"

Xavier laughed while shaking his head. "You're so beautiful, Dinah."

"Do not shower me with compliments, especially if you think you're gonna get something in return." Dinah said taking a drink from her lemonade.

"Dinah." He paused. "I really wanna know why you think so cruel of me. Is it the looks, the lifestyle, I mean what is it?"

"If I thought you were so cruel, trust me, I would not be sitting across this table from you."

"I really wanna know how you really feel. I don't believe that you were giving me your all on our little walk."

"I rather not, talk about it."

"Okay." Xavier put his hands up. Whatever you say, Dinah." At that point the waiter was bringing out their food out.

"So, how the studying been going?"

"You want me to be honest with you?"

"If you're not, don't even speak."

"Honestly, I haven't even cracked open a book yet."

"So, you haven't studied, and you have a placement test in like two weeks?"

"I mean, I know it sounds bad, but that's one of the main reasons why I need your help. Who wouldn't pay attention, if you're assisting them."

"Let me think about it."

"C'mon, help me out. I'm stupid, this is some shit I should have been learned like in the first year of high school. All that algebraic equations, variables, polynomials and whatever else I gotta get good at."

"Don't talk like that."

"I'm just saying, I'm a hood guy, that's dumb as hell and fell into the stereotype of young black dropouts."

"Xavier, you're not dumb. Everybody learns differently. You may be good at another subject. You're trying, that's all that matter. You said you wanted to sign up for the classes, right?"

"Yeah."

"Well, saying that you signed up and got accepted into the program to even be able to take the placement test, is accomplishing a goal of yours and that sound pretty damn smart to me."

"You right, I didn't look at it that way."

"You learn something new every day."

"If you can't help me because you have to finish your school work with still juggling everything you been through, I'll understand."

"Don't worry, I can scooch you in. How about tutoring sessions via skype or facetime on Tuesdays and Thursdays from 6:15 to 7:30pm."

"Sounds like a plan. Thank you so much Dinah, you don't know how much this means."

"You're welcome, just make sure you on time when calling in."

"Talking about be on time."

They continued with their conversation, talking about where they wanted to be in their personal lives within the next year and what goals they were reaching for. They were enjoying their food as well as each other's company.

"It feel like I been knowing you forever, girl."

"How's that?"

"I don't know. It's just something about you."

Ding. Dinah's phone sounded. "My cousin, just texted me making sure I was good, so I think I should heading back."

"Okay, let me pay and we can be on our way."

Dinah walked out the diner before Xavier, so she can start the car. Before getting in, Xavier wrapped his arms around her. "You're my motivation." He said before walking to the passenger side. Dinah enjoyed his time and company, but she wasn't feeding into all his compliments. Genuine or not. It was hard for her to let her guard down now. Coming to the diner with Xavier alone, was enough considering how her mind was set up.

***

It was hitting on 1:30 in the morning when Desire and I got back in the house. Uncle Judah was sleep. We tiptoed up the stairs into Desire's room, we laughed as we put on our night gowns in haste.

"So, where did you and Mr. Man run off too?"

"We rode up to the diner."

"How do you know this guy?"

"We met last year at University of Glenview."

"Aw okay, he doesn't look like the college type."

"When I met him, he was trying to sign up for GED classes."

"GED classes!"

"Shhh' and yes, GED classes, that's when he offered me to help him."

"Well, it looks like you offering more than tutoring services."

"Desire, it aint even like that, trust me."

"So, he's a bad boy."

"Desire!" I gave her a side-eye.

"What…Look, I'm just saying, a person may be known by his looks and if it looks like a bad boy, talk like a bad boy, walk like a bad boy then it's a bad boy."

"Girl, whatever."

"Don't get side tracked, Dinah."

"Don't get side tracked says miss, oh daddy were just going out to eat and going down town to do some sightseeing."

"Hahaha, girl go to sleep don't try to run that game on me." Desire responded.

***

It was about 2:30 in the morning and we were just leaving the party. We decided we were gonna crash at Rodney's crib.

"Bro, where you was at?" Kenny asked.

"X aint even gotta say nothing, I saw him talking to a fine little piece outside of the set." Jermaine added.

"X wasn't even in the party for all of forty-five minutes before he dipped off." Rodney added.

"I find it really funny, that y'all mogs are talking about me like I'm not sitting in the passenger seat right now."

"We're just saying bro, you was gone for a lil minute. I know you got something during that time."

"Dinah aint that type of girl, we just hit up the diner on Woods and Taylor."

"Bro, so you mean to tell me, all y'all did was grab a bite to eat?"

"Yes, bro. I just told you that's not how she get down."

"Don't tell me ole girl turning you soft, bro."

"Boi, you already know aint no softness in my blood."

Chapter Thirteen

An Ordered Hit

"So what you trying to do?" Terry asked Jamal as they both looked out the car windows, checking their surroundings.

"Look, Jeffro already gave us the rundown," Jamal responded. "His cellmate ordered a hit out on this cat named Xavier, but not a hit to kill, he want him to feel this heat."

"Man look, I'm tryin' to earn my stripes."

"Terry, just give me the piece, before yo ass mess around and have us both in jail for murder. If we don't follow orders, Jeffro will have a hit out on us."

"You right, you right." Terry realized. "So do you wanna roll up on him or do you wanna get out and handle it?"

"You one bold negro." Jamal said to Terry. "Look, let's switch gears. You drive and I'll handle him."

After switching gears, they saw Xavier walking in the opposite direction from the gas stations with a bag of chips, an Arizona iced tea and a scratch off in his hand. Once he walked thirty feet past the car, they made sure their masks were on and loaded. Terry let the windows down and did a U-turn causing the tires to screech.

When Xavier heard the sound of the tires, he looked back and instantly started running.

Jamal with half his body out of the window, fired. *Pow Pow.Pow,* is what you heard as shots fired from Jamal's gun. Xavier's items hit the ground right along with his body.

Two shots aimed straight at Xavier, Jamal didn't miss. Once Terry and Jamal saw that he was down. They knew they had completed their task. They began driving fast, getting out of the jam, nearly hitting other cars in the process.

"Damn, man!" Jamal said as he took off his mask.

"What's up." Terry asked while still driving fast.

"I think it's over for him."

"What the hell you mean, what you do?"

"I think one hit buddy in his back."

"Nigga do you think or do you know?"

"I don't know, man. I just was trying to pop him in his leg and send a message like Jeffro said." Jamal said with his adrenaline rushing.

"Man, yo ass is slow. Jeffro bout to be on our asses."

***

"Victim is a black male, in his early twenty's, about six feet tall, medium complexion. He has been identified as Xavier Wells." The head nurse said to the nurses on the side of her and behind her as they pushed the gurney through the emergency room.

"Man, I hope that young dude is okay." A man said as he looked at his wife. The couple didn't know Xavier, but by the younger generation having a no-snitching policy, when the ambulance and police arrived at the scene everybody was looking dumbfounded, so the forty year old couple Mr. and Mrs. Rhodes, who were sitting on the porch the same time the shooting took place, stepped up and offered to go to the hospital with him.

"Is that his phone." Mrs. Rhodes asked her husband.

"Yeah, I took it out his pocket before the ambulance got there. I'm gonna see if I can call someone in his contacts."

The last person, Xavier tried calling was Dinah, so that's who Mr. Rhodes dialed.

Chapter Fourteen

AN EMOTIONAL CALL

"Okay class, your Lab reports are due at 11:59 on Sunday. You all are dismissed." When Professor Buchanan said that, it was like music to my ears. After I get some Chipotle, all I wanna do is rest. Xavier wanted me to start tutoring him after our talk two nights ago. I guess I can see that he's serious about trying to get an education. But, we were gonna have to start another time because I was tired and didn't plan on seeing another book or assignment for the rest of the day.

Ring, Ring, Ring. Speaking of Xavier, he's calling right now. I can just tell him we will pick up tomorrow.

"Hello." I said with a slight smirk, reminiscing on our deep conversation the other day.

"Hello, do this happen to be Dinah?"

"Umm, yes. Who is this?"

"Miss, my name is Mr. Rhodes and we picked up this phone at the scene of a shooting."

"What." I said as I paused and put my hand over my mouth. "Do you happen to know the name of the victim?" I asked hoping they didn't say Xavier's name.

"Xavier Wells, ma'am."

"Oh my gosh, I'm on my way." I ran to my car.

Heart pumping, head racing, tears nearly about to fall down my face. I didn't understand how this just happened, like we were just together talking about goals and how he was going to get his life back on track with going to school and everything. I was driving 80 miles per hour. Trying to get to Hope Valley Hospital as fast as I could.

"Hello, do this happen to be Dinah?"

"Umm, yes. Who is this?"

"Miss, my name is Mr. Rhodes and we picked up this phone at the scene of a shooting."

That was the only thing that kept playing back in my head while on my way to Glenview. I couldn't believe I just got a call saying that Xavier was shot, and I couldn't believe that I was driving over three hours to make sure he was good. I know Xavier and I was just picking up the pieces to our friendship or whatever, but I knew I couldn't leave him hanging like that.

When Mr. Rhodes said that over the phone. I felt like everything went blank. All of a sudden, feelings for X began to arise and I didn't know where it was coming from. Knowing that he have a crackhead for a mother, a father that lives on the other side of town and his buddies trailing behind trying to be the top seller. I felt like I was the one who genuinely cared.

Two hours enroute, I called Xavier's phone back to see if Mr. Rhodes had an update.

"Hello, anything on Xavier?"

"The doctors said they are working on it, I believe they are about to perform surgery on him."

Tears began to roll down my face more. I felt like this was my fault. If I wasn't waving him off for so long and just helped him get into school sooner, he wouldn't be in this mess.

I pulled up to Hope Valley Hospital at about five o'clock in the evening and headed straight for the emergency room.

Scoping out the people in the emergency room. I only saw one older couple, so I assumed it was Mr. Rhodes with who appeared to be his wife.

"Hey-- Mr. and Mrs. Rhodes?" I assumed.

"Yes, Dinah?" He asked as we shook hands.

"Anything on what happened?"

"Well we were on our porch during the time of the incident. We were enjoying the afternoon breeze and suddenly, we heard tires screeching. My wife and I saw the victim, Xavier running and a guy with a mask on tilted out the window pointing towards him. He shot him in the leg, but Xavier still tried to get away, so he shot him again and that bullet went straight for his back. After the car sped off. I ran over to the scene and called the police."

"This is insane, why would somebody do such a thing." I responded in a crackled voice.

"If you don't mind me asking, are you his significant other?"

"No, we're just friends." I replied.

Trying to leave that topic, I asked, "Did you call anyone else.?"

"I called a number under Mom and Dad like five times, but no one answered, so I left a voicemail letting them know what took place. I also called some people under the name of Kenny, Jermaine, Rodney and Cruze. One of them picked up and said they will be here once they round the rest of their crew up, but I haven't seen anyone here for Xavier so far, but you." Mr. Rhodes said shrugging his shoulders.

"Do you live near here?"

"No, I'm almost three hours away headed west."

"Well, the doctors couldn't give information out to people who wasn't family, so I told the nurses and doctors that me and my wife were his uncle and aunt.

Just as he was explaining that, a nurse was walking up to where we were sitting with a clipboard in his head.

"Uncle and aunt, right?" The nurse remembered.

"Yes, sir. Is he okay?" We all stood there waiting for his response.

"Xavier Wells is in stable condition. We managed to get the bullet out of his leg, and the second bullet only grazed his lower back, but when the bullet hit his back it sent his body through a physical shock. So, with a few weeks of monitoring and physical therapy, Mr. Wells should be back to his normal self.

"How is he right now?" I asked.

"He's pretty tired. You guys can go see him if you like. Only one guest at a time. But I must tell you, he may go in and out. The medicine from his surgery has not worn off, yet.

"Thanks so much." I said.

"Well, you gon' on in there to check on your friend." Mr. Rhodes said. I found it nice that somebody who don't even know Xavier was by his side until somebody who knew him showed up.

I dreaded the elevator ride to Xavier's room. I stood outside the door of room 428. I had to mentally prepare to see X under these conditions. His curtain was pulled back so when I did turn to see him, a tear fell. Although he looked like he was sleeping peacefully, I didn't like how they had him hooked up to machines and an IV and other needles stuck in his arms.

I walked in and stood over him, looking at the machine and making sure nothing was off. I touched his hand softly as I sat down in the chair next to his bed.

Oh my gosh, I hope them fools don't do nothing crazy, I thought, just realizing that Mr. Rhodes said Jermaine was gathering their whole crew up. I turned to Xavier as our eyes met.

"Dinahhh." He said dragging his words and his eyes barely open.

"Yes, it's me. I'm here for you ok, just get you some rest." He grabbed my hand tighter.

"You shouldn't have come all the way out here for me." He responded with his eyes close and a slow speech.

"Xavier, please get you some rest, don't worry about me." It was knocking on 7:30 at night and I knew it would be 10:45 by the time I got home. I sat there for a little while longer, just to be that support for him.

"Xavier, I'll be to see you, if not tomorrow, the day after."

"You--you leave -leaving me?" He responded, again with his eyes closed as his voice stuttered.

"Yes, but trust me, I'm gonna be back up here." I said

getting up from the seat. As soon as I got towards the door, Xavier was knocked out. I hope he gets well soon because these hospital drugs will really do a number on you.

Chapter Fifteen

JERMAINE AND THE CREW

I was gathering the crew up. Some man called talking about somebody shot X. I mean like, what the hell. Do people really wanna take it there? All I know is I was ready to get on that with anybody who had something to do with his shooting. I just hope they aint take my mans out, on the real. I can't deal with losing any more guys to gun violence.

Ring Ring. "We outside, let's go." Once Rodney gave me the call. I hopped in the car and we were on our way to Hope Valley.

Once I got in the car, our buddy Cruze sped off. All the guys were in the car and we wanted answers.

"Now, how you here about what happened to X?"

"Some man name Mr. Rhodes come calling me from X phone asking if I was Jermaine and if I knew Xavier Wells. I knew something was up because he said bro whole name.

So, I'm like yeah that's one of my guys, what's good? Then that's when he told me he was in the hospital shot up with some gun wounds."

"Man, I'm ready to go on a mission. I mean get the niggas who did this and the niggas that know them. I'm hitting anybody." Rodney said.

"Man, if Tim wasn't in jail, he would be on it in 0.5 seconds." Kenny added. He always think Tim could save the day.

Thirty minutes later, we hopped out the car ready to get the who, what, when, where and how's to this whole situation.

"Where the hell our buddy at man." Rodney said causing a scene as we walked in the emergency room.

"Are you looking for Xavier Wells?" The man Mr. Rhodes approached me.

"Yeah, you who I spoke with?" I asked.

"Yeah, the doctor said he's in stable condition. He just got out of surgery not too long ago, he mentioned that he might be going in and out for a while from the medicine. His friend Dinah is in there with him now."

"Thanks sir."

"No problem. Now that his loved ones are here, I think it's a good time for me and my wife here to head out."

"Well, thanks again, sir. If it wasn't for you, we would

have never known what was going on."

"I called who I could. You guys have a good night."

Once the man left. I wanted answers. Hell, we all did. "Excuse me miss nurse lady. Do you have any info on a Xavier Wells?"

"Hold on sir, let me see."

Ten Minutes Later.

"Okay, so Xavier Wells is stable, but right now were only allowing one guest at a time. Someone is up there right now, so once they leave, you're more than welcome to go up to see him."

"Thanks for that info ma'am."

Chapter Sixteen

CRUZE'S MISSION

See, I'm Cruze. Me and Xavier are super close. I know y'all thought Jermaine was his right-hand man, but we were more like brothers. Our fathers were best friends, so that's how we grew up. Blood couldn't make us no closer. See, when y'all first got introduced to Glenview and the guys, I was locked up, so y'all didn't hear about me.

Jermaine and the crew wasn't amped up enough. I had the type of attitude to shut things down on the people who did this and their loved ones. These niggas tried to take my brother out. Bets believe I'm gonna find out who did this and that's a guaranteed.

I couldn't sit in this emergency room too long. I need answers and info. I left out the waiting area and walked to the front of the hospital. I had to get some fresh air, before I caught another case.

"Detective Kohl speaking."

"What's up unc? I need a favor." I said as I checked my surroundings.

"I wanted a favor from you too, that was to stay outta jail and you couldn't do that."

"Unc, you think I wanted to go back?"

"Yeah, Yeah. What's this favor you claim you need?"

"Ok, you remember Terrance?"

"Yeah, him and your daddy was real tight."

"Right, Right, so that mean you remember X?"

"Yeah, I remember X. Where you getting at?"

"Okay, somebody tried to take bro out. I'm at Hope Valley right now and I need you to get a license or surveillance on who did this."

"Cruze, do you think I'm a crook?"

"Look, Uncle Kohl, do this for me and I promise I got you."

"I don't know, because if I consider looking into some stuff for you and give you the slightest of info, you gonna do some shit to get put back in jail plus that's jeopardizing my job."

"Nahh unc, I'll make sure nothing gets back to you. I just wanna show mogs – Don't come for none of my guys in the View and think were not gonna find out about it."

"Cruze, get off my line. I'll see what I can do, bye."

Damn, my uncle was on some B.S. What's the point of having a job like that if you can't help your people out? I knew my uncle was hard to deal with at times, but let that would have been one of his old buddies calling for a favor, he would have been flying to get info, but for me, he thinks I'mma do something off the wall. He'll be calling back, even if I have to keep reminding him. Uncle Kohl gonna give me some info on these fools.

"Where you was at?" Jermaine asked as I walked back into the hospital.

"I was trying to get eyes on the niggas that did this. You wanna live by the gun, you must don't mind dying by it."

"Yeah, I'm thinking the same thing."

"What, I'm trying to figure out, is if y'all ass became punks when I was locked up."

"Bro, what the hell are you talking about? You going off for real."

"All I'm saying is we should be making moves right now."

"Bro, calm down, you think we don't want to render pay back to the mogs who did this. I know I do, but we're trying to check on bro first."

"I understand that, but the longer we sit down—it just makes it easier for them to get out of dodge."

"Well, let's see what X wants done to the ones who did this."

***

Kenny knew some female that worked at Hope Valley. He said she was gonna let all us go up to Xavier's room, but only for twenty minutes. That's how long she was going to be on that floor.

She came down and all of us rode the elevator to the fourth floor. "Kenny, I'm gonna text your phone when the twenty minutes over. Y'all don't got but one visitors pass, so I gotta take y'all back down."

"Thanks Tisha, we appreciate it." Kenny said before we approached the room.

Xavier was just opening his eyes, when we walked in. "Brooo, you alright? How yo leg feel? Jermaine asked.

"A little numb right now. How all y'all ass get up here at once?"

"Xavier, you worried about the wrong shit right now, we need to know what happened and how it happened." I responded.

"Look, I was coming from the gas station, minding my own damn business. Something in me felt a little off track, but I didn't pay it know mind. So about one minute later, I look back again, and I hear tires screeching as the car did a U-turn. I knew the car was coming towards me, so I start running, next thing you know I feel something hot hit my leg, but it didn't get me all the way down, so I feel something skirt across my back and after that I was out."

"Bro, hearing that just make me wanna, do something reckless." I said as I cuffed my palm.

"On the real." The other guys chimed in.

"Look, I don't know who did this shit to me, but they was trying to take me out. I can tell you one thing though. Tim was behind this."

"Bro, you sure you not doped off the medicine." Rodney asked.

"Yeah, bro. I don't think he would be on that with you." Kenny agreed.

The guys didn't believe Xavier, but my bro know what he's talking about. I'mma take his word for it, but the question is who he have to do this? We was his only guys.

See, that's why I need my uncle to use his detective skills. I need him to see how many calls been made, to what number. Check signs of code language, check for license plates, surveillance. Who that car is registered too, that did the shooting. What connections they got with somebody in the same prison Tim is in. I need all that and when I get that info, it's lights out.

Chapter Seventeen

DON'T BE REPROBATE

I made it in the house around 10:30 at night. My dad was sitting on the couch watching the news.

"Dinah?" He stopped me right before I went upstairs to my room.

"Yes, daddy." I turned around with one foot still on the stairs.

"Where have you been?"

"Huh? I asked in a confused tone, not wanting to tell him that I was just in Glenview.

"You heard exactly what I said."

"Daddy, what are you talking about? I just went to school and hung out a little."

"Yeah, with who?

"Daddy." I whined.

"Don't daddy me, now I know your thought process

haven't been the same lately, but I hope you not trying to change that boy."

First, how do he know this and secondly, really what is my dad talking about?

"I hope you don't think you can change him. If you do, you must have a reprobate mind because you can't change nobody but yourself."

"Daddy, this boy that you're talking about didn't do nothing to me. All he wanted was my help and I'm not trying to change nobody, but if he came looking for a change. I know I'll be able to assist."

"Okay, since you wanna say that. If you let a negro cause you to fall too far from the laws I taught you, you don't have to worry about staying here. You can go stay with his ass."

"Daddy, I will never fall off." I said in an honest tone. It was the truth though. My dad didn't always see stuff from my stand point. Plus, this so-called lecture he giving me right now was just his strong drink talking. I saw the bottle of Hennessey Pure White that he got from the Caribbean sitting right on the table half empty.

"You heard what I said, don't be going out of your way for nobody that's not going to do the same for you. When you do good know to whom you do it for."

"C'mon now daddy, I know that."

"Okay Dinah, if you say so, but don't be playing the

middle, that's what we call lukewarm and one more thing before you go to your room…. I know you and Desire went to a party and I know you left during that party and who you left with. I'm saying that to say this, think about that before you do something, I got eyes in the city. Anything you do, nine times outta ten, I'm gonna hear about it. I'm not raising no hoes in this house, you hear me?"

Where were those eyes last year, when I was forced into Tim's escorting service?

"Now, come give your daddy some love."

Muah. I kissed my daddy on the cheek. "Good night daddy."

"Good night, my daughter. It's all in love. You're daddy one and only baby girl." He said as he gave me a kiss on my cheek. "Go get you some rest now."

"Thank goodness." I sighed as I sat on my bed, today was a long day. From going to school, to driving to and from Glenview.

I showered, put my hair in a messy bun, threw on my Love Pink night gown and fuzzy sock before snuggling up under my cover. This was the cure to my long day.

Laying my head on my pillow, caused me to drift off in the daze. But before I could day dream about my future, my phone began buzzing. Can't be nobody but Desire.

Nope, I was wrong. It was Xavier.

Xavier: Hey what's up?

Me: How is it even possible that you're texting me?

Xavier: Dinah, I got shot in the leg, not the head. You acting like I can't still function.

Me: You funny, but I still wasn't expecting you to be on the phone.

Xavier: I'm only on the phone to text you. I know they practically had me doped up off that medicine, but I wanted to tell you that I appreciate you. You being one of the first faces I see when I open my eyes from surgery really showed me you down for me, you really care about me. You the real MVP, Dinah.

Me: Thanks for such kind words, I wouldn't leave you hanging like that. I'm just glad you're okay.

Xavier: You know I had to be strong for you.

Me: Lol, talking about you had to be strong for me. What you doing anyways?

Xavier: Waiting on them to bring me some food, they got a 24-hour cafeteria in here and I'm like super hungry

Me: Aw okay, whatever they bring you. I hope it satisfy your hunger.

Xavier: Girl, you don't even have to be talking about school and you will still sound smart and well educated.

Me: Hahaha. I can't deal, but you were going in and out when I was there. I was trying to tell you, I was gonna try to make it up there tomorrow. If not tomorrow, the day after.

Xavier: Okay, sounds like a plan, I look forward to seeing your pretty face.

Xavier and I continued to text all night, until I went to sleep. He must stayed up through the night, because I kept hearing my phone vibrate, but couldn't keep my eyes open to view anything on my phone. I just said forget about it and went to sleep.

Chapter Eighteen

WORD ON THAT HIT

⎯⎯⎯ ∞ ⎯⎯⎯

"What's word on that hit?" Tim asked Jeffro.

"Oh, you know it's done, I told you my guys had that handled. Xavier Wells, right?"

"Yeah."

"Buddy in the hospital. When the guard came to get you for your visiting hours, I saw it on the news in the break room. He got hit in the leg and a bullet slightly grazed his back. So, he aint dead, we just taught him a lesson. You don't ever come talking out the side of your mouth to some big shots, especially one that took you in and took care of you." Jeffro went on.

"I like the way you think. You took the words right out of my mouth."

"Bro what you all happy for." Jeffro noticed more than just a light smirk.

"One of my girls, who used to work for me just came up here to visit, she told me she was low on funds. I told her she can still work for me while I'm in here. I told her she can keep her cut and hand me up the rest, so it can go on my books and other needs."

Jeffro gave Tim dap. "See, that's another example of having your name ring bells from the cell. We still making money. Lawrence county prison system can't stop us."

"Yeah bro, you can get in on this too. If you know any guys from the Rockwell projects who need someone for a party or just too... you know. Let me know, every guy you send to me for her I will share the funds with you."

"Okay, cool. I'll put a word out."

***

I can't believe I just agreed to business with Tim, again. I feel like I have fell into his trap once more, but it's been hard for me. I was low on funds and the only person who had connections to me making fast money was Tim.

This was only supposed to be another friendly visit, but it turned into business after me confessing the low estate I was in. Tim explained how he would link me up with some legit people. He said as long as I agreed to give him 60 percent of my earnings we had a deal. He made it sound so good. On a good day if I made 2500 dollars, Tim will get

1500 and I'll keep 1,000. That's just the type of income I need every other day to get on my feet and get things done.

I've tried to look for jobs, I tried to get back in school, but all because of that little charge on my background, nobody was trying to accept me or hire me, so I had to do what I had to do. I don't know how my uncle will take it, if he finds out about this, but I was focused on making money.

Tim had me driving a 2016 Tesla MX last year, so why would I go back to riding the bus, Tim had me bringing in at least 4800 dollars a week, so why would I settle for a paycheck of four hundred dollars every two weeks. I guess I got use to a certain lifestyle with him and I had to maintain it. Well, at least that's what Aunt Shayna thinks.

Chapter Nineteen
THE RISE OF TIFFANY

I didn't know Xavier was in the hospital. I feel bad knowing that he's been there for three days and I haven't been up there to see him, yet. I gotta go show my face. It's the least I can do.

My name is Tiffany. Xavier and I use to kick it about three years ago, but he dropped me like a bad habit when his friend accused me of something I didn't do. I feel sorry that he got shot and I was willing to put our differences to the side.

"Adrienne, can you take me to Hope Valley." I dialed my best friend.

"Is everything okay, what's wrong?"

"You remember Xavier?"

"Of course, I remember him. You know how many times you kept me up all night talking about him."

"Girl, the good ole days, but I just found out he got shot and he's at Hope Valley."

"Oh my Gosh, are you serious. What happened?"

"I don't know, but I wanna show my face, you know show him that I still care."

"Uh ohh. Is someone trying to rekindle an old flame?"

"Adrienne, I'm not about to deal with you. Are you gonna take me or what?"

"Yeah, I'll be to get you in a little while, but are you sure he wanna see you, y'all stop talking on bad terms."

"I don't care about all that. I just wanna make sure he's good."

"Okay, I'll be there in about thirty minutes."

***

Tiffany and her friend Adrienne walked into Hope Valley and signed the visiting list and sat down waiting to be called.

Ten minutes into their wait, Dinah walked in. "I have some food for Wells." Dinah walked up the front desk as she displayed the bag of food.

"Hold on one second ma'am." The nurse said as she checked something on the computer.

"Girl, look, look." Adrienne nudged Tiffany as she was watching "The Real" talk show on the hospital TV.

"What?"

"Who's that girl? Because delivery workers don't dress like that."

"You right, that's a good question and he damn sure don't have a sister."

"Okay miss, you can go up," The nurse gave her a visitor's pass.

"Ohh, hell nawl, I'm about to see about this." Tiffany got up and walked up the front desk. "Excuse me, how did that girl get to go up before me when I was here first?"

"Ma'am, she's on Wells immediate visitation list and he's expecting her at this time."

"Immediate visitation, what's that?"

"That means some people are listed as priority visitors and some people are listed as regular visitors.

"Aww okay, I guess." Tiffany rolled her eyes and walked back over to her seat.

"What they say?" Adrienne asked wanting to know the scoop.

"They talking about she's on his immediate visitation list and I have to wait till she gets done. I'm most definitely about to find out who she is."

"Jealous much. "Adrienne chuckled.

"Jealous for what? Me and X was three years ago. Like I said, I'm just here to show my face." She fronted. Tiffany was indeed showing signs of jealousy. Her seeing Dinah walk in with her all white flowing dress with the gold pleated belt, hair in the wet-n-go style, glitter rhinestone open toe sandals that complemented her fresh pedicure that matched her manicure. If it was a competition, she knew it would be hard to compete.

***

"You really got me something." Xavier said as he saw Dinah walk in with a bag.

"Yeah, I told you I would. I got you some jerk chicken, cabbage, sweet potatoes and red beans and rice." Dinah said as she handed him the bag.

"Dang, you just set me up right." He said while opening the tray and sniffing the aroma.

"Yeah, I got you something that I know gonna fill you up, I also got you some Nike shirts and basketball shorts, just in case you get tired of wearing those hospital gowns. The nurses can help you get up and put it on if you need too."

"Thank you, thank you so much. You don't know how much this means to me."

"You're welcome. My pleasure." She said while twirling her keys.

"Why you standing up? Sit down. Talk to me."

"I actually can't stay long today. I have to handle some

business. I'll try to stop back this way later, but I doubt if I'm gonna be back today.

"Aww man, you know I enjoy your company."

"I know, but I gotta head out. Enjoy your food."

"Okay, I'm gonna call you later." Dinah left Xavier room and took the elevator down towards the front entrance. After returning her visitors pass she felt someone eyeing her, but didn't pay it much attention. When she got well into the parking lot Tiffany and Adrienne ran over by the automatic door to see where she was heading towards.

"She's driving a clean 2017. Ole girl must got a little money. How Xavier pull that?" Adrienne said as they watched Dinah get into her car.

"Adrienne, you saying that, like I'm not on nothing."

"Best friend, now you know she don't got nothing on you." Adrienne geeked Tiffany head up while walking back to their seats.

"You got that right." Tiffany said giving Adrienne a hi-five.

"Ma'am you can go up now." The nurse said while writing Tiffany out a visitors pass.

"Thank you."

"Hey, Xavier." Tiffany said as she peaked her head in the door before entering. Xavier instantly gave her the stale face: One, because she interrupted his eating and two, because she was the last person he wanted to see. "Why you look that, are you okay?"

"Yeah, I'm straight. Just trying to figure out what you doing here?"

"Damn, I can't come check on you?"

"Like I said, what you want?" Xavier responded while flipping through the channels.

"Damn, you still got a cold heart, even after getting popped."

"See, it's that kinda talk right there that make me dislike you."

"I'm saying. Why you acting like this towards me?"

"You know why I'm the way I am towards you. Let us not forget what you did three years ago."

"Whatever, you can't prove it."

"Tiffany, I'm not about to go back and forth with you."

"X, I don't have time for your attitude, but one thing I wanna know is; who is ole girl?"

"Hahaha." Xavier laughed. "Do it look like I have to explain myself to you?"

"I see she got you eating good."

"Yeah, and your point?"

"I mean, I just wanna know who she is."

"She aint you."

"Most definitely not, she don't have nothing on me."

"Tiffany, don't flatter yourself."

"Whatever, I just came to show my face."

"And you did, now you can go."

"That's how you— you know what, bye Xavier, I don't have to take your shit."

"Well, get the hell out of my room, then." Tiffany stomped out of the room waving Xavier off. She rode the elevator down the stairs furious with how her visit just went and everyone that looked at her could read anger all over her face.

"That look don't look like everything with well."

"Adrienne, let's just go." Tiffany responded walking towards the door.

"Tiff, what happened?" Adrienne ran behind Tiffany because she was pacing out of the door.

"Girl, he just sat up there and treated me like I was a piece of crap."

"Well, did he say who that girl was?"

"Nawl, he talking about she aint you, but that's okay though. I'm gonna find out who she is and when I do, she gon' know who Tiffany is."

Chapter Twenty

HARD TO COME BY.

"**B**ro. I need you to do something for me." I hit up Cruze.

"What's good, bro?"

"Now, don't laugh at me."

"I got you. What's up? You beating around the bush, X."

"Do you have something decent in your stash?"

"I'm sitting on something."

"I need you to get me a necklace, with Dinah's name engraved; one of those bar necklaces."

"Alright, I can get it done. You really like this girl huh?"

"Aye, they don't make them like this no more. Her type is hard to come by. She don' brought ya boy dinners, Nike fits. Aint nobody ask her to do that man, she just did it."

"Aye, bro. I hear you. If I found a nice girl who had the smarts, the looks and was down for me. I wouldn't let that go neither." Cruze said. I knew my bro would understand.

"For a minute, I thought you was gonna try to clown me."

"Nawl, aye man. I get it. Just can't be about that life and have nobody to hold you down."

"You a fool, Cruze."

"Just know, when y'all get married, this fool is gonna be the best man."

"Talking about marriage, we haven't crossed that line yet, but see if Jeremy the Jeweler can have that done, by like tomorrow."

"I'll see."

"Aww, I almost forgot. Guess who had the nerve to come up here."

"Who."

"Tiffany."

"Bro, after she don' came on to Rodney's cousin behind your back, she had the nerve to show her face."

"That's what I'm saying. I treated her ass all the way out of my room. Then she talking about you can't prove what I did."

"Something is wrong with that girl, she acts like she wasn't sending Rafael letters in jail under another name."

"Right, but enough talking about that harlot. See if Jeremy the Jeweler can have that done for you." I said reminding him. "Cruze, I need real gold. Not nothing fake."

"Ya bro got taste. I'm actually not too far from Jeremy's spot so I'm gonna head up there in a little while.

Chapter Twenty-One
RACHEL'S NIGHT OUT.

I t was my first night out. I had a three-day line up. Tim most definitely know how to put in some calls. How you a business man from jail. Probably one of the reasons why I kept falling into his trap. Tonight, I was going to be working at a mansion. Tim had me connected with a senior executive of MVP records. All I can say is money, money, money, mon-nay.

A few days ago, Tim had me meet up with some guy who wrote me a check for 3,700 dollars with my name on it. It was so I could get me a nice little wardrobe and to rent a car to get around in. Now, it wasn't a Tesla MX, but I wasn't on the bus neither.

Tonight, I was going with my signature look: Hair flat ironed bone straight that fell at my shoulders, nude lipstick, black calf-length dress and black heels. I had the house all to myself. Well, almost. Aunt Shayna and I was the only ones' home. I put on my sneakers, so it would look less obvious where I was on my way too. After putting my heels in my purse. I slipped on a nice mid-length trench coat and made my way towards the front door.

"Where you about to go?" Shayna asked.

Damn, how I'm about to pull this one off.

"I'm just about to go hang out with—"

"Aww, look at you all dolled up." She stopped me in mid-sentence as I turned around to answer her. "Well, go make you Mon—I mean, go have fun." She smiled.

She thought I didn't catch that. I made it to where it wouldn't be so obvious. How could she possibly know where I was headed to?

After, I said goodbye to Shayna. I walked out the house and walked three blocks south. It was no way I was parking this car in the driveway of my uncles' house. I hopped in the car, before starting the car and pulling off, I paused.

Rachel, now go do what you gotta do and get out of there. I said my thoughts aloud.

I pulled off with one goal in mind and that was to make enough money. Five minutes into my drive. I started to feel uneasy. A voice kept popping in my head, but it wasn't me. I tried to shake it off, but it kept popping up. Was this my intuition?

"Rachel, what are you doing? Isn't this the same thing that got

you locked up the last time? Ask yourself-- would you rather have fast money and no dignity, or would you rather have a little money, but have self-respect."

I shook my head and kept driving. I couldn't let that voice get to me. I cut the radio on max, to drown out the voice. It was no turning back. All I had was ten dollars to my name the last time I went to visit Tim. My plan was to make a little money to do what I needed to do and some.

I pulled up to tall double black gates. I rolled down my window and pressed an intercom button.

"Hello, how may I help you?" A women's' voice greeted.

"Yes, it's Camille K here for Tevin Matthews." I responded. Tim told me to go by Camille K, just in case the police came to shut down somewhere I was working and wanted answers.

"Come in, Mr. Matthews is expecting you. The greeter buzzed as the double gates opened. I drove through the lot, where I saw a fountain with water falling so calm and beautiful. I parked and walked up what felt like thirty stairs to get to the door. This time I buzzed the doorbell. I was greeted by what sounded like a different lady who greeted me through the intercom. When I looked to my right there was another lady, who appear to be a maid, standing there with a tray, with a shot of Cîroc and when I turned to my left there was another lady standing there, with a tray of chocolate covered strawberries. I took a shot of Cîroc and placed the glass back on the tray, then took a chocolate covered strawberry.

Mr. Tevin really know how to treat his guest.

"Camille K, Mr. Tevin would like you to meet him two doors down. After the greeter directed me, I entered the room.

"Camille, Camille, Camille. How are you?" Tevin Matthews stood up from his desk and kissed my hand.

"I'm fine."

"You sure are, Tim didn't tell me that he had something like this on his hand."

"Well sir, how will you like your night to start?" I asked. Even though I was amazed by the greeters and the fancy complementary drinks and strawberries. I was here to make money and leave.

"I would like for us to get in the pool first."

"Well, I really didn't want to get my hair wet."

"How about my Jacuzzi then?" He asked.

I agreed. We proceeded to the Jacuzzi and after we talked, I followed him to his room. It wasn't anything grand, like I thought due to the fact how my welcome was. I did what I had to do and left; with 3,500 dollars that is. Biggest amount I ever received from one client. I got in my car, counted my money and then my phone rang.

"Hey, Camille K?"

"Um, yes." I responded knowing it was Tevin. How did he get my personal number? I wondered.

"How did you get this number?"

"I always get what I want." He replied.

I knew it was something to this large amount.

"I suppose, what's up?"

"I enjoyed how the night ended, and I was very much so interested in you. How about you come work for me?"

"Um, I don't know."

"Look, you'll be granted your own guest home, a consisted amount of funds for your personal needs, a higher percentage than what you getting and a way better car than what you're driving."

That all sounded good, but this could be some kinda game.

"Sorry, I don't think I can take you up on that offer."

"You do realize that you're working for someone who has twenty five years in prison, right? It's your loss though."

He had a point, but it was better this way.

I refused to live with somebody I barely knew, with all that fancy stuff. I know y'all thinking, you lived with Tim and you barley knew him, but that was different.

"Rachel, is this really the life you want to live. Do you want to live in a house with five other women, who's under subjection to a man, that got them caught up? Do you really think that those women are just maids and greeters who signed up for the job?

"Oh my gosh." I said as I slouched back in my seat. It was that voice popping up in my head again, but this time I actually paid it some attention. What if those women were actually forced into their positions? What if those women were just coming over one night for a good time and one by one he hit them with the call like he just did me? What if they fed into it and it wasn't all what Tevin said it would be and there in the position they're in now; trapped.

This voice had me conflicted. I had to get out of here. I zoomed out of his parking way. Let me just shake this off and get out of dodge. Money is still to be made, but I most definitely won't be coming back here.

Chapter Twenty-Two

Too Caught Up

"I'm back." Dinah said as she approached my room, looking good with her Dupointe University shirt and jean skirt with those things that hang off the bottom of it that matched her nail polish, looking all educational with a lap top bag that went over her shoulder.

"No text, no call. Just surprise huh?"

"Yeah, today was my early day at school, so I figured I come up here." She said as she down beside me. "Did they say how much longer you were gonna be in here?"

"Just two more days, they want to monitor me a little longer, then it's two weeks to rehab I go.

"Then you'll be back to normal, huh?"

"You already know."

"Let me see the remote, because it doesn't look like you watching nothing good." She reached for the remote and flipped through some channels until she saw Law and Order SVU pop up on the screen. While she was so into the show, I took this as the perfect time to talk to her and tell her how I really feel.

"Dinah, I'm sorry I wasn't all the way up front with you about what I was into last year. You know with dealing drugs and being in that lifestyle."

She turned my way. "I understand. I mean I was a little upset at first, but I forgive you. Apology accepted." She turned right back to the show as if I wasn't trying to have a serious conversation with her.

"I just feel like I steered you in the wrong direction."

"X, we are good. Everything happened the way it did for a reason." She said before looking up at the television again. I'm starting to think she's trying to avoid this conversation.

I figured while she was all up into the TV, I could present the gift I got for her. I bet you this will grab her attention. I reached over and grabbed the golden box that had a bow wrapped around it.

Damn, how am I about to do this. I never felt this way about no female.

"I got something for you."

"What you got for me?" She said as she turned around with a smirk on her face. I knew that would grab her attention.

"Here, open it up." I handed her the box.

"X, how thoughtful." She responded with the biggest smile on her face. "Oh my gosh, Xavier, this is beautiful, and it has my name engraved. Thanks so much. I don't know what to say."

"Let me put it on for you." She bended down, so that she could meet the height of the bed. I rose up a little, moved her curls out the way and snapped it on.

"What made you do this for me?"

"Look Dinah, you been down for me since day one. You saw potential in me, when I didn't see it in my damn self. That's why I wanna know why you playing with me?"

"What are you talking about?" She asked in a confused tone.

"I'm talking 'bout us. Isn't it a reason why we're doing all of this?"

"X, it's not like that. I'm just you know—helping you out as a friend."

"Dinah, how long you gonna keep singing that same song?"

"I just—"

"Let me finish, because I don't think you realize. When I was naked, you clothed me, when I was thirsty you gave me drink, while I'm sick, you coming to visit me and when I was hungry, you fed me. So, you who I really want to be with."

***

Dinah knew that Xavier was telling the truth, but she couldn't muster up to say it.

She knew for a fact, her and Xavier could never take things to the next level. Her parents would laugh her to scorn. They didn't believe in the boyfriend—girlfriend phase. They believed in the good ole courting stage. You know; being involved with someone formally and romantically, typically with the intention of marrying them.

"Xavier, I care for you too, but--."

"So you just going to keep denying your feeling, huh?" He stopped her in her tracks.

"I'm not. I'm just scared. Will everything I worked for, not work out? How will my parents feel? Am I ready for the emotional attachment that you give? Are these really my true feelings or am I just vulnerable?"

"Dinah how long are you gonna keep living in the shadows of your parents? Don't get me wrong. I can tell they did a damn good job at raising you and teaching you the right way. I wish I had that in my life. I'm tired of living the way that I have. I been in this lifestyle since I was ten, Dinah. Ten, do you hear me. Getting shot in the leg only, just showed me that God really spared my life. They could have taken me out, if they really wanted to." Xavier expressed, shedding a tear. He didn't want Dinah to see him like that, but he felt

112

like he could be himself around her. She just gave him a hug as she laid her head on his chest letting her emotions out.

Chapter Twenty-Three

TOO MUCH

"Woooh." I let out a sigh. I was on my way home. I didn't know Xavier felt that way about me and I didn't even realize I felt a certain way about him. Where did I go wrong? It's not supposed to be like this.

Honestly, I don't know where all these feelings came from, but, all I know is that I needed to clear my mind. I vowed to myself that I would be all work, no play this year. No relationships or friendships that would cause emotions to run deep. Life has a funny way of changing your plans though.

If my parents or my brother knew that I was visiting Xavier, they would go into an uproar. They would start thinking that he's going to take me away from everything they taught me and this and that; y'all know the rest.

See, I knew Xavier had a genuine heart, he just became

a product of his environment and that's hard to get away from.

"Hey mama." I ran in the kitchen and gave her a big hug. I finally caught her without it being late at night or super early in the morning. Ever since my dad said she didn't have to work, she's been out and about. If it's not retail shopping, its grocery shopping, if it's not grocery shopping, she out getting another item for the house.

"Hey, my daughter, why you just give me a hug like a big kid?"

"Because, I miss you mommy." I said in a kid's voice, playing.

"I know, for about the past week or so, we would only see each other if we were on our way to bed or early in the morning."

"I know right, I haven't had a chance to invade you and daddy's bed and just talk to you."

"You funny, D. Why you look like that though?"

"Like what?"

"It's only, 3:30 and you look exhausted."

"I'm good, it might just be school overtaking me." I played it cool.

"Aww okay, is that a new necklace I see? Where you get that from? It's just glistening and sitting pretty." My mom noticed. Just as my mom said that my dad was walking up the stairs coming out of the basement, or his man cave; that is.

Dang, can I talk to my mom by myself for once. If I could, she might be able to help me with this predicament I'm in.

"A friend got it for me."

"Just know a gift destroys the heart, Dinah." My father chimed in.

"Yeah, if you let it."

"Levi, why you have to go there, how you know who brought it for her." My mom said as she gave him a kiss before she went back to the counter to cut her vegetables for dinner.

"Thanks mom." I chuckled in agreeance.

"You got me a lot of gifts, when we were proving each other, babe. I didn't destroy my heart, it made it even better." My mom said with a little laugh.

"That's why you my rib." My dad said as he grabbed her hand and pulled her in for a hug and a peck on the lips. *Here they go.* "But, Dinah here, is a different story, you can't compare her to us. I'm not gonna lecture her though, she's grown."

"Right and I'm sure she knows right from wrong." My mom responded. While they continued to be all lovey dovey. I sat in the living room and cut on the TV, Lifetime movie network should clear my mind.

Chapter Twenty-Four

HIGH SCHOOL MEMORIES

———⟨∞⟩———

"Mortgage is paid, bills is paid." Levi said to himself walking out of the bank.

"Levi Israel, what's good with you?" A man said from the opposite side of the lot. Levi paused, having to bring the face back to remembrance.

"Deonte Kohl, Sherman High. Class of 1992." Levi said as they greeted each other with a brotherly hug.

"Dang man, the last time I saw you was about four years after we graduated high school." Deonte said.

"Yeah, that was, what—1996."

"Yeah, it's been a long time. What you doing around these parts."

"I live not too far from here."

"What?"

"Yeah, it's a long story." Levi said, knowing that that topic was not up for discussion.

"Partner, I don't have nothing but time, come grab a bite with ya old buddy, man."

"I got a little time, where you trying to meet at."

"How about Roscoe's Restaurant and Bar?"

"Alright, I'll meet you there in about ten minutes."

Levi and his old high school buddy, both got into their cars and was on their way to Roscoe's.

After they met up and got seated. They ordered a couple of beers and some wings while getting caught up.

"So, you don' came up. Deontae Kohl is a detective." Levi joked.

"Yeah, you know I had to turn my life around and do better for myself."

"I feel you, bruh. I had to do the same."

"I see, you a family man now, huh? I remember when we--" Deontae was interrupted, due to his phone ringing.

He declined the called and continued. "Like I was saying. I remember when we both was making moves in Glenview.

"Man, we were young and didn't know any better." They both laughed.

"Aye, you remember when my mom got me that 1990 Jeep Grand Cherokee. We had all the females on our heels when we pulled up in that thang." Deontae shook his hand memorizing.

"That was the era of the high top fades, starter jackets and classic Jordan's." Said Levi

"Hold on, nigh. You remember how we was able to afford that?"

"Aww, Deontae, here you go. Don't start."

Man, we was taking over the projects. I mean Glenview, Rockwell, Lawrence county, Metro county, Decatur town, Ktown. We were everywhere. If it was popping, we was there trying to make a quick buck."

"Man, you just opened up a can of memories, that's the 90's for ya."

Ring, Ring. Deontae phone rang again.

"Tae, you might wanna answer that, or you gonna hear a lot of nagging from your wife." Levi joked.

"Nawl, my wife is out with her friends. That's my big head nephew hounding me down; He want me to look into something. One of his little buddies X, got shot about a week ago and he want me to get eyes on the guys that did it."

Levi took a drink of his beer. "Young cats, nowadays. Where this happen at?"

"Over there in South Glenview."

The puzzle pieces started flowing through Levi's head. He heard the name X, and knew it had to be Xavier. He knew if the story got far enough, somehow some info was gonna come up and trace back to his daughter's name.

"So, what you gonna do, detective?" They both laughed.

"I don't know. After he called the first time about it, he called back with more details. Apparently, X went to check some so called big shot in jail, told him off and said he wasn't working for him no more. My nephew Cruze say he was defending some girls' honor that he likes."

"Damn, man. That's messed up." Levi expressed. He knew that the girl Detective Kohl was speaking of was Dinah, but he wasn't gonna say it. Levi wanted to see how everything will play out.

"Off that, though. How about you? Did you ever marry that one female, that you said will be the one to change you? Even though we was off ripping and running the streets, she stuck by your side."

"Yeah, Tamar. That's my wife, we got two kids together, one boy and one girl. Been married for over thirteen years."

"Look at you, I knew you could turn into a family man." Deontae said. Although he was talking, his words were fading out to Levi. He went into deep thought.

It had just dawned on him that his nephew is calling about the same guy that he's been trying to stop his daughter from seeing, and the so called big shot was Tim, the same guy that he and Simeon checked and laid hands on. It also dawned on him that Dinah was the modern version of the younger Tamar; her mom, and Xavier was the modern version of the younger him. This conversation had conflicted him and something had to be done.

"Man, nice talking with you, buddy. I gotta be heading back." Levi said talking a last swallow from his beer.

"I need to be heading back to the city my damn self. Aye, keep in touch, bruh. Be safe out here."

They gave each other a pound and pat on the back and went their separate ways.

Chapter Twenty-Five

OLD COMMUNICATIONS

“T’man, I need you to get some answers for me.” Levi made a call.

“What’s up, old boss? Tell me what you need.”

“What you know about this cat named Xavier?”

“You talking about Xavier from Glenview, everybody calls him X?”

“Yeah, that’s exactly who I’m talking about.”

“I mean I heard his name in the streets a few times, he had some little work here and there, but the last time I heard his name, they was saying he got shot.”

“Umm, really, so do you think he’s gonna eventually get back out on the streets.”

“Possibly. From what I heard, he only got shot in the leg, so if it didn’t hit no main vein, he should be back out in little to no time, it’s too much money to make in Glenview, especially with their leader being in jail.

"Right, Right. Look, if you hear his name in anybody's mouth or see him. Let me know his moves and the 411 he into."

"Got you, when you coming back into the business?"

"Never. I left that alone a long time ago and you need to leave that life alone too."

"Look, I'm young and I gotta keep my father's legacy going."

"Yeah, I don't think your dad meant what he said, but keep me posted on that info."

Levi had to go outside of the puzzle and get factual info before he had another mission in place. As you can see, he was once in that lifestyle before getting married and having children. He made it out; seeing how dangerous and crazy it could get. That's why he's so firm with Dinah.

He know guys in that lifestyle would love a pretty girl like Dinah on their arm, but will use them for what they can do for them at the same time. Levi refused to let that happen to his daughter.

Chapter Twenty-Six

GUESS WHO'S BACK

I was laying low; giving it some time from seeing Xavier. I don't wanna be any distraction to him while he's in Physical Therapy to strengthen his leg. Surprisingly, me doing that, cleared my mind.

"Hey Dad, Hey Simeon." I spoke as I walked in through the back door. I placed my keys on the kitchen counter and my bag on the table.

"Hey Dinah." I heard a deep voice say. The voice was all too familiar, but I was still unsure of who it was. With a glass of lemonade in my hand, I took two steps back peeking into the living room.

"Jeremiah?" I smiled. This has to be a dream, right now. I haven't seen this guy in a long time, ever since he and his family went to California.

"Dinah, guess where Jerimiah is transferring too." My

dad said with a grin on his face. A grin like he was up to something, but I didn't know what.

"Where?"

"To Dupointe."

"Oh, really. So, you moving back huh?" I asked, joining them on the couch.

"Yeah, Cali was cool, but there's no place like home." He responded as he smiled my way.

"You got that right." My dad agreed.

"Soo, Dinah. Can we hang out sometimes?"

So he's really gonna ask me that in front of my dad and brother?

"Of course, y'all should go hang out on the town, do some catching up." My dad spoke for me. He was definitely up to something.

Let me give y'all the back story really quick. Jeremiah and I was close. Our parents were always together. You know: My dad and his dad, his mom and my mom. So, we were always around each other. Our parents noticed a little connection between the two of us and said when we get of age, we could start courting. This was all put in place when we were fifteen years old, but shortly after, his parents decided that they were gonna move, so his father could help build in Cali. It broke my little heart, but now, he's back. Like, he's really back and were not underage anymore. Oh my, what else could my young adult life go through?

"I don't know. I will have to check my schedule."

"She don't have nothing to do after she gets out of class, trust me her schedule will be clear."

Dad, really.

I hope my dad don't think Jeremiah can just come back to the city and everything is just gonna be all good how it use to be, Jeremiah will have to earn my interest back and that's if I allow to even happen.

"Well, Levi. Simeon. Good talking with y'all. I'm about to head out." Jeremiah said as he got up and gave them a pound.

"Dinah, think about." He looked my way, with a charming smile.

"Will do." I said as I continued to browse through my phone.

Once Jeremiah left, my dad came back into the living room, listing out his stats.

"Jeremiah, has grown to be a strong young man."

"Yeah." I responded nonchalantly.

"I thought you would have been happy to see him."

Ohh, so now it's not a problem, because it's Jeremiah, huh?

"I mean, it's good he moving back to the city, but you can't just be offering my time and whatnot."

"Dinah, what do you really have to do once you get out of school? Nothing." He asked me a rhetorical question.

"How I see it, he's the only one I will allow you to prove and have a courtship with. He's respectful, he keep the laws, he got a good head on his shoulder and his parent's raised him on the same core values we raised you on. I know he won't get you into no trouble, he's gonna do everything accordingly to keep his good name."

"So does that automatically makes us a match?"

"Dinah, I'm your father. I know what's best for you."

"I suppose."

"Daddy, you know she don't be saying all that when she's riding to Glenview."

I rolled my eyes. "Simeon, shut up. You get on my nerves—you know what, I'm gonna ride around and finishing cooling off. I sit here and try to have a nice sit down with my family but look how that turns out. See y'all. I'll be back later."

I removed myself from the living room and got in my car. I was just all over the place. Too much was going on in my little life once again. From trying to balance school work, emotions, getting over last year's situation, and with Jeremiah being back; it just threw a whole mix into my equation. I decided to hit up Desire to let off some steam.

"Desire." I said in an overwhelming tone.

"Dinah, what you up too?"

"Desire, I been going through it and if one more out

of the ordinary thing come up in my life again, I'm gonna burst."

"Spill the 411."

"Okay, so you remember Xavier, right?"

"Yeah, that's crazy how he got shot right after we seen him." She added.

"Right, so you know. I've been helping him out a little, you know little clothes and food while he's been in the hospital. I figured it was the least I could do, you know. His mom is in rehab trying to get herself together and his dad is on the other side of town. So, after we talked at the party and diner. It was like a little connection. Do I want it to be? Not nessacarily, then, emotions started coming out of nowhere. Next thing I know, my daddy come talking about he got eyes in the city and he know we went to the party and who I was talking to at the party."

"Girl, we need a girl's night, because you stuck between a rock and a hard place."

"I'm telling you, but that's not the rising point; I went to see Xavier again, you know being a friend or whatever you call it and while I'm watching TV, he presents me with this gold necklace with my name engraved and then he got to talking about how he wanna change and how I been there for him since day one. So, now I'm like do I deny these little feelings or what?" I paused.

"Why you stop? Carry on, this is like a movie."

"Girl, because just talking about it is overwhelming. Now, Xavier is in Physical Therapy, so I'm like, I'm gonna take a little break from going to see him. So, today I walk in the house and I speak to my daddy and Simeon. I came in through the back, so I poured me a glass of lemonade and all I hear is, "Hey Dinah." Girl, you won't believe who it was."

"Who? Who?" Desire said hyped up.

"Jeremiah."

"Wait, wait. The Jeremiah who your parents and his parents said that they wanted y'all to court once y'all turned eighteen, but he ended moving to Cali.

"Yes."

"Damn, Dinah. This is a tough situation."

"I know right and he already talking about can we hang out. I'm thinking like, you leave when we were fifteen years old and just think we can have the same connection at twenty-one."

"Dinah, but you know Uncle Levi would never approve of you and Xavier."

"I know, but I feel like he trust in me now. Like, we have built loyalty."

"But, cuz' you gotta remember too. You and Jeremiah parents already had y'all decided. They had y'all life planned out. I remember: Y'all was gonna start proving and courting at eighteen and after a few years of courting if everything worked out, y'all was gonna be prepping for marriage. That's how your parents do, his parents do and how my parents— well my dad do." Desire paused right there, she always got a little down when speaking about her mom. Her mom left their house because she didn't want to abide by any of her father rules and didn't want him to lead and be head over the house. "Are you okay? I've been so caught up in my situation, I never asked you how you was taking that?" I asked.

"I'm good. Carry on." She responded, waving it off.

"Okay, I mean, knowing that he's back is exciting, but it's like where was he at last year during my difficult time."

"So, what you're gonna do, because face it. We're growing up and I know we have been rebellious at time, but our parents only want what's best for us. I mean we have seen some good righteous marriages take place. Now, were just waiting on our turn. Don't you want somebody to take care of you? Lead you? Do right by you and build you up?"

"I mean, yeah that's what I want."

"Well, if that's what you want, then Xavier is not it."

"So you're saying, give my connection another shot with Jeremiah."

"Yeah, that's exactly what I'm saying. I know Xavier probably seemed cool to you, but really cuz' he was just filling a piece of the old you."

Desire was dropping some knowledge. What she was saying was right. I just had to accept it.

"Still, I'm not gonna be hasty to start proving Jeremiah because he's back."

"Dinah, you acting like y'all just met."

"Okay, so how I suppose to just stop talking to Xavier?"

"I can't help you right there D. You got yourself into that situation and you're gonna have to get yourself out."

"Ughhh." I banged on the steering wheel in frustration.

"You'll figure something out. I know you will."

"Thanks for the advice, Desire. I'm about to go grab me a bite to eat and then ride around til' I get tired."

"You're welcome. Call me back later."

"Alright. See ya."

I'm glad I called my cousin. She really made me realize that, maybe seeing Xavier was unhealthy and that it will profit me no good. My thing is, how do I suppose to just stop? Do I call and let him know? Should I shoot him a text? Do I wait til he's done with physical therapy or should I just wait til' he contacts me?

Chapter Twenty-Seven

NIGHT GONE WRONG.

Today was gonna be different. It was day three of my line up and after this one, I will be waiting for my next rounds. The first night getting back out was crazy, especially with that voice that kept popping in my head, trying to stop me from making money.

My second night was the normal, nothing too fancy. Just did what I had to do, got paid and left. Tonight, was probably gonna be the same. Now, the guys I was meeting tonight didn't have no corporate job or big savings, but what they did have was fast money. I was meeting with a guy from the Rockwell projects; let's see how this goes.

It was just me at my uncle's house, so getting ready should be smooth sailing.

Aunt Shayna convinced me to get some weave in my hair, so tonight's look consisted of an 20 inch wavy Indian

Remy weave, pink sheer lipstick, a dark blue dress and heels.

After getting ready, I walked to the car. I put the address into my gps and was on my way. Surprisingly, when I pulled up, it was a club, the "Raven" night club.

Good thing I didn't have to be in the projects.

"I'm here for Kayno's event." I approached the security.

"You?" The security asked while looking at me as if I was some kind of model or something.

"Yeah, me."

"Gon' right ahead. The VIP section will have a banner that says Kayno." The security watched as I walked in.

When I walked in. It was half way packed, but it wasn't even ten o'clock yet, so I knew that was gonna change in about an hour or so.

My 20 inch weave swung as I walked up the stairs where I was approached by some guy. "Damn, who is you?" He asked in a flirtatious manner. It was clear that he didn't finish school, speaking to me like that.

"I'm Camille and I'm looking for Kayno."

"Aye, Kayno. Ole girl looking for you."

"Jeffro aint tell me she was that bad." I heard him whisper to his buddy before coming to greet me.

"So you Camille, huh?" He said while putting his hand on the wall leaning into my space.

"Yep, that's me." I responded, looking around.

"Well, I got word that you good at what you do. Right now, I just need you to follow my lead. Being on my arm for this party and then a little later we can get outta here."

I sat in VIP with Kayno and his buddies. They were popping bottles, laughing, drinking, sending girls up and sending girls down as well as getting drunk. Kayno asked me to dance for him, over in another section of the VIP, I did. But soon after, I felt hot and had to make sure my hair and make-up wasn't sweating out.

"Hey, I'm gonna go down to the restroom. I'll be back." I walked down the stairs to the restroom. The one with the stalls were filling up, so I went to the single restroom instead.

***

Aye Kayno, what you're waiting on to get into that?" Jarvis asked referring to Rachel, well, Camille.

"She look good, don't she. Jeffro referred her. I was gonna wait till later on, once I got outta here." Kayno responded.

"If you keep drinking the way that you are, there's not gonna be a later on for you. You already a little tipsy right now."

"Where she go?" Kayno asked.

"She said she was going to the restroom. I saw her go into that single one though."

"Oh, yeah."

"Yeah, that's why I'm saying go handle that. Matter of fact, I'll go down with you, just to make sure she doesn't try nothing."

"Yo, Shawn, Jamal, Terry and Buck, me and Kayno will be right back." Jarvis let some of their guys know before heading down the stairs.

***

"Okay my hair is still together. Shoot, it better be. I paid over 300 dollars for this weave, make up still looking good, dress looking goo-"

Knock, Knock

"Somebody's in here." Rachel responded to the banging on the door.

Knock, Knock.

"I said somebody's in here—" Both Kayno and Jarvis walked in the single restroom.

"I know you was in here that's why I came."

"Okay, is it something that you want?" Rachel asked in a confused matter.

"Yeah, don't play."

"Play—what?"

"Jarvis, I can take it from here. Be my eyes and my ears, stand outside of the door until I come out." Kayno explained.

"Ohh hell nawl, you're on some other shit and you're drunk." Rachel said as she tried to get pass Kayno to the door, but he pushed her into the sink.

"Why you playing me girl?" He asked as he grabbed her and pulled her close to him.

"Stop. Let me go." Rachel said as she hit him in the chest.

"Didn't you come here for me? You think you're just gonna walk in here looking all good, dancing and all that shit and expect me not to react." Kayno said as he began to pull up her dress. Rachel kept fighting it.

"Stoppp. Let me out."

"Don't fight it, aint this what you do anyways?" He asked as he cut off the lights. He covered her mouth and told her to be quiet. He was man handling her, nearly ripping her dress apart.

"You gonna give me some." He put his hand around her neck and took full control. Kayno was on her too strong. Strong to the point where it was impossible for Rachel to get out of his grip.

Meanwhile on the other side of the door

"You next? That Vodka got me having to go." A local clubgoer asked Jarvis as he approached the single restroom.

"Nawl, my homeboy in there, he messed up. He in there throwing up and all that. I'm just blocking the door, being his eyes and ears."

"AAAH...."

"You sure everything good in there?" The guy asked as he heard faded out screams from the other side of the door.

"Yeah, that goose got him loose. Got him an upset stomach and as you can see he's regretting that shit now." Jarvis lied.

***

Just take it. Don't resist." Kayno said while on top of her.

Rachel laying on her back in a dusty restroom, with her head turned, tears flowing and nose running. Not trying to look Kayno in the face. She began to hit him in the chest, trying to fight one last time, but that did nothing but made matters worse.

He grabbed her neck tighter while forcing himself in to her even harder. She just wanted it all to be over at this point, she didn't want any money or anything. She just wanted to get out and run.

Kayno let go of her neck as he finished up with her. He stood up and shook off his ripped shirt, before leaving out.

"Man, we gotta go." Kayno said to Jarvis.

"Man, what the hell did you do in there? What about the guys? The party?"

"Look forget that. We gots to go." Kayno said as he

grabbed him as they moved through the crowd and left out a back exit.

Rachel still laying on the restroom floor with her legs trembling tried to get up, but she stumbled. She was unstable. When she did finally get up with tears still wailing her eyes. She only had one heel on and her dress was ripped showcasing her bra. She opened the restroom door, wiping her nose and ran out of the side exit. She took off the one heel she did have and ran. She stumbled a few times, but she didn't stop.

Now, about twelve blocks away from the club, she looked up at a sign that said – Grace Hospital: 1 mile south- after seeing that she ran south until she touched foot on the hospital's property. She walked in the Emergency room where she yelled. "HELP. I'VE BEEN RAPED." As she fell down in the middle of the emergency room floor.

The nurse that was at the front desk. Called in some more nurses. The head nurse called the security guard that was on duty. They came rushing out from the back as they picked her up, put her in a wheelchair and rolled her to the back. They placed her in a room, gave her some water and a gown to put on. She sat there still trembling as she played back the events in her head.

"Hello. Miss. May I ask you your name?" The nurse asked. Rachel didn't answer as she sat there in silence.

"Okay, well I'm Nurse Gruwell and I'm going to ask you a few questions, is that okay?" Rachel still didn't answer. "Okay, I'm going to give you a little time. I'll be back shortly."

Rachel was sitting on the hospital bed, thinking about what she had got herself into. Then, suddenly her phone rang. What a coincidence, it was Tim.

"You have a collect call from -- Tim. If you choose to accept this call, press one."

"What's up, you done with your night at the club already?" Tim asked.

Rachel sniffled. "Tim, I was raped."

"Raped, are you sure?"

"Yes, in the bathroom of the club. I don't know where you found this client, but you don't have to worry about me ever doing this shit again."

"Rachel, I need you to calm down, take a breather, get some rest and get back to work. You can't let this affect you."

"What the hell is wrong with you? Are you sick? What part don't you understand, I'm not doing this shit no more."

"Rachel, don't do this."

"Don't do what? All you care about is your damn self. You don't care if I get hurt, raped or ran over as long as you get your ends. I don't know why you even called me. Find somebody else to do your dirty work. Goodbye."

Chapter Twenty-Eight

KOHL AND LONNIE

"Lonnie and Kohl I need y'all to go to Grace Hospital, they have a rape victim in custody."

"Sergeant, I'm working a case."

"And you can work on that case, when you get back, but I need you two to head over to Grace, now."

Lonnie and Detective Kohl were on their way to Grace. Lonnie wasn't a detective, but she was known to be a damn good female cop.

"Kohl thinks he's too good to ride around with an officer." She said as she opened the driver's side door. "Don't forget you was just in uniform a couple of years ago, patrolling the streets."

"You damn right and I worked my ass off to become a detective." He laughed, knowing that Lonnie just wanted to hear him talk.

They pulled up to Grace Hospital, ready to ask questions. "Kohl, you ready to see where this investigation takes us?"

"I wouldn't call it all that, but I guess."

"Excuse me, miss. My partner and I was called in to speak with a rape victim."

"Yes, right this way." The nurse instructed them to follow. "The victim came in, dress ripped like she had to fight someone off of her, hair a mess. When she came in she fell in the middle of the emergency room, breathing fast. You can tell she was trying to flee her attacker. There she goes, she haven't said much, maybe you two can get through to her."

"Thank for that info." Lonnie replied.

"Hello, I'm Officer Lonnie and this is Detective Kohl. Can you tell us your name?"

Rachel just sat there on the hospital bed, biting her bottom lip while rocking back and forth.

"Miss, were on your side, can you give us your name?"

"It's Camille-- Camille Kasier." She opened up as Detective Kohl wrote it on his notepad.

"Okay, Camille, now, can you tell us what happened?"

She sniffled. "I was in a nightclub, with a few of my friends. After a while, I had to go to the restroom. The restroom that had multiple stalls were filling up fast and had a line. I noticed a single restroom and that it was empty. While I was making sure my makeup was good, a guy came in with another guy. It look like he had a little too much to drink. I asked the guy what he wanted. He told his friend to look out for the door and then he locked it and that's how it started."

"Do you know the guy name?"

"I think his name was Kayno."

"You think?" Detective Kohl asked. Lonnie knew Kohl was a little skeptical of the story she was airing out.

"How do you know the guy name was Kayno, did you have any interactions with him?" Lonnie asked.

"I mean, I talked to him for a while, like a friendly guy at the club."

"Okay, give me and my partner a second." Lonnie excused her and Detective Kohl from the room.

While walking down the hallway Lonnie asked. "Kohl, what you thinking?"

"I think she's escorting or prostituting herself."

"Kohl, you can't say that about every decent looking girl from the city that says they've been raped, you heard what the doctor said about how she came in here."

"Man, look. I can tell by her whole countenance. Her appearance and look tells me that it's more to this story."

"If it is more to the story, why would she say she was raped?"

"I believe that she was selling her body, whoever she was dealing with didn't pay up and now she's crying rape."

"It's only one way to tell."

Lonnie and Kohl went back to the car to look up the name "Camille K-- she told them the K stood for Kaiser. When they searched the name Camille Kasier, a lady who was charged ten years ago, for helping with a drug cartel popped up. Kohl felt even more suspicious of the story, because only one Camille Kasier, was in the system.

Lonnie stepped out of the car, due to a phone call. Detective Kohl knew something wasn't right, but he decided to look into some info his nephew Cruze gave him.

"Tim Edwards." He whispered as he typed it into their system on the computer. Conviction: 25 years for Kidnapping 20 year old girl, running underground escort ring. Alliances: Tyrone Lemons; Rachel Davis. Kohl already knew about Tyrone Lemons from years back, but what stood out to him was that he had a women on his team. Kohl was curious, so he clicked the name.

Lo and behold, Rachel picture popped up. Kohl was shocked and surprised he wasn't expecting to see the innocent girl sitting in Grace Hospital to pop up on the screen.

Kohl tapped on the car window to get Lonnie's attention. "You're gonna wanna see this."

Lonnie hopped back into the car and began reading off

the priors. Rachel Davis: Served one years in Metro County Correctional Facility; Co-conspiring to kidnapping, Escorting.

"What the hell, how you find this?"

Not saying to much he said "I looked up a name my nephew gave me and I just so happen to see a female name pop up as one of his alliances and boom so called "Camille K" pops up."

"I guess those detective skills are paying off, huh."

"Yeah, now, let's bring her ass in for questioning."

They walked back into the hospital and went to Rachel's room. The looks on their face read "We mean serious business."

"Camille K, can you tell us what really happened."

"I did tell y'all what really happen. You want me to keep reliving that same scene in my mind?"

"Well, since your ass wanna be smart, we know your name is not Camille Kasier. Yeah we did a diligent search on your ass, Rachel Davis." Detective Kohl responded.

Rachel sat there in shock, as if she didn't know what they were talking about.

"Rachel Davis, you're under arrest for giving false statements to an officer, anything you say and do can be used against you in a court of law." Officer Lonnie read off her Miranda rights as she cuffed her.

"What the hell? Y'all police system is screwed the hell up. I'm the one that's been raped, but y'all cuffing me instead of the Nigga that did this to me."

The nurses were confused to what was going on. "Nurse Gurwell, is it? Can you call District 31 and ask for Detective Kohl or Officer Lonnie when you get the lab results to the Rape Kit, thanks."

They placed her in the back of the car, ready to head down to the station.

"Your ass just got out of jail for escorting less than six months and now you're back out her doing the same thing." Kohl ranted.

"I'm telling the truth, why you don't believe me?"

"Because, if you will lie about your name, what else would lie about?"

"Okay, my name is not Camille Kasier, but I was raped."

"Un huh." Lonnie answered.

"Look I know I have a history, but I'm telling the truth." Rachel cried.

Officer Lonnie and Detective Kohl listened to her cry and plead all the way until they got to the station.

They put her in the interrogation room. Detective Kohl was taking over at this point. Lonnie, Sergeant Ticks and their Lieutenant Dager was listening from the other side. Lonnie had gave them the rundown on how everything took place so they were interested to see how this was going to play out.

Detective Kohl walked back in the room with a folder. "What's your connection with Tim Edwards?"

"What do he have to do with this?"

"Answer the damn question."

"He's who I was dealing with before getting locked up."

"That's not what I'm talking about."

"Well, I don't know what you're talking about."

"You know what, you got a real smart mouth-- apparently Tim name is out in the streets again. He put a hit out on someone."

"Look, I don't know anything about any hits on anyone."

"Oh really, because here, records show that you went to visit him less than a month ago."

"I went to see him for a friendly visit, not to set no one up or put a hit on anyone."

"I think you're lying and if you're withholding information, we can charge you with that shooting. So, if you don't cough up any info on something-- you looking at five years. How that sound?" Kohl gave her a grin.

"Okay. Okay. I went to visit Tim, I was low on money so he said he still had some contacts on him that could give me an easy payout. I took him up on the offer. I went to "The Raven" nightclub. He said it was a guy named Kayno from the Rockwell Projects who was having a party. I was supposed to look pretty on his arm, then I was supposed to do my part when we left. I got hot, so I told him I was going to the restroom--"

"Stop, right there. You said Rockwell projects."

"Yeah."

"Tell me some of the names you heard, while at the party."

"Umm-- Kayno, Terry, Shawn, Jamal, Lenard."

"Okay, proceed."

"So, I told him I was going to the restroom. I went to the Single restroom, because the one with the stalls were filling up fast."

"Wait-- so why others didn't go to the single restroom, before you?"

"The single restroom, had said occupied, but when I looked down under the door, I noticed the light was off, I knocked and didn't hear anything, so I let myself in. I used it and washed my hands. After that, I began fixing my hair and making sure my makeup was good. That's when I heard a knock, before I could fully say who is it, Kayno and his friend came bursting through the door. He told his friend to wait in front of the door and to be the lookout. I told him, we were supposed to wait till the club scene was over. He said "Why would you come in here looking all good, if you didn't want to be touched." After that he grabbed me, I tried to get away, but he was strong manning me. He cut off the lights and pushed me down to the floor. After that he took control and raped me."

"That story seems almost real."

"It is real, you still think I'm lying. You really think I'll make up something like that."

Knock Knock. Lonnie peaked through. "Lab results came back, you're gonna wanna see this."

"Hold on one second." Kohl said as he walked out of the room.

"We do have semen samples that matches Karvell "Kay-no" Wilson, 24-years old. 3581 south Albany."

"That's the Rockwell Projects" Detective Kohl responded.

"Right and he could be tied to the Albany Block Boys gang."

"Let's go lock his ass up."

Chapter Twenty-Nine

WE'RE HAVING COMPANY.

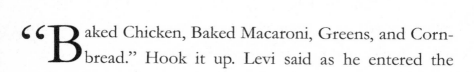

"Baked Chicken, Baked Macaroni, Greens, and Corn-bread." Hook it up. Levi said as he entered the kitchen.

"You know I am. I'm about to get this started now." Tamar responded.

"Where's Dinah?"

"Upstairs, taking a nap. You know she got a week off from school."

"Yeah, well she needs to get up and help you."

"I'm fine, my love. I know school be weighing on her."

"She still could help, two are better than one. It gets the job done."

"You right, I'm just so happy to finally see my friend again." Tamar said referring to Jeremiah's mom, Leah.

"Yeah, I'm glad my bro James is back in town." Levi replied referring to Jeremiah's dad.

"You think Jeremiah is happy to see Dinah?" Tamar asked while seasoning her chicken.

"The question is; is Dinah happy to see Jeremiah?"

"What you mean?"

"Well, when he came to visit the other day, she walked in and she smiled at him, but when he was talking to her she was being real stand-offish."

"What was that all about?" Tamar asked. "I don't know, but she's been going to Glenview, being so-called friends with some guy. I aint having it no more. She will not get caught up as long as she's in my house."

"I'm in agreeance with you on that. I refuse to let something happen to my baby again." Tamar shook her head. "Are you still standing on your word from six years ago?"

"You talking about Dinah and Jeremiah courting?"

"Yeah."

"I think he will be the perfect fit for Dinah. We know his parents, we know how he was raised, and we know that he'll lead Dinah down the right path."

"Yeah, I agree; because she's not getting any younger. We got married at 21. If James and Leah is on the same page as far as them two proving each other for marriage, then the faster we can get them out of our houses." They both laughed.

"It is about time we have the house to ourselves." Levi replied.

"Children free house, please."

"Don't worry, honey. That time is coming."

"Speaking of time. What time is the house of James coming?"

"Around 7:30, I believe."

"Good, my food will be done around 8:00."

"Yeah, I was gonna go get us some beers and get you and Leah some wine coolers, later on. Until then, I'm about to go check on Dinah."

"Levi, now you know she's gonna be upset with you, if you go up there trying to wake her up."

"Guess what, I don't care, because I'm the daddy." He joked.

"You a trip." After Levi and Tamar finished their conversation, Levi walked upstairs.

Knock. Knock.

"Who is it?" Dinah yawned.

"Your daddy."

"Aww…," She paused. "Come in." Levi opened the door.

"You been sleeping for a mighty long time."

"Finally got a break from school, I figured I could catch up on a little sleep."

"Un huh." He said as he sat in her computer chair. "Dinah, I need to talk to you."

"Okay, I'm listening." She said still laying in her bed.

"I'm about to be real with you. I have given you a lot of lean weigh. If you're going to the city to see that Xavier dude, it ends today. It's not safe and the situation he's in is not safe."

Not denying it, Dinah said. "How do you know all of this?"

"Listen, I ran into one of my old high school buddies. He's a detective and he have a nephew that's friends with Xavier. His nephew is trying to get eyes on whoever did the shooting. I don't know where my old buddy Deontae head is at, but if he give his nephew the slightest info; he's gonna run with it and with that comes retaliation, a lot of back and forth shootings, police investigations and possible deaths." At this point Dinah is at the edge of her bed, in shock to the info that she's hearing. "I see how you looking Dinah. I say all that to say. I'm trying to keep you out of harm's way, so it ends today."

"Wow, dad. I would have never known. Thank you so much. I'm sorry for being rebellious and not listening to what you say."

"Apology accepted. I know I have to be longsuffering with my daughter."

"Aww, I love you daddy." Dinah said as she gave him a hug.

"I know, love you too."

"I'm gonna go to the store in a minute, at some point go down stairs to see if your mom needs help with anything. The house of James is coming over."

"Jeremiah gonna be here?" She smiled while stretching.

"Of course, he's gonna be here."

"Alright, thanks again dad."

***

All I can say is wow. Glenview is big, but it's small. How my daddy know somebody that know Xavier; crazy, right? On the other hand, my dad seems pretty serious about calling me and Xavier's friendship quits. But, I gotta admit, I'm happy he gave me that info. Now, I just gotta let Xavier know that we can't have a friendship anymore. This is gonna be hard. I have to mentally prepare myself for the response I may get.

I searched for his name in my phone and fixed my fingers to send out the text.

Hey Xavier. Hope Physical Therapy is going good for you. I'm not gonna be able to see you anymore. My dad doesn't approve of our friendship. He told me that as long as I'm under his roof that rule applies. Sorry I have to break this to you. If I'm in the city and I just so happen to see you around, we can speak and be causal. But as far as spending time, I won't be able too. Hope you're not upset.... Best Regards.

Whoo. Sending that text was harder than my 10-page psychology paper, but it had to be done.

I got up off my bed and opened my laptop. Grades were in and I had to check.

"Business and Entrepreneurship: A. Intro to Micro Biology: B. That class is hard anyways. Abnormal Psych: A. Music 121: A. Three A's and one B. Sounds like a scholar to me." I said aloud to myself.

Now let me get downstairs to see if my mom needs help before Jeremiah and his parents get here.

Chapter Thirty

THE HOUSE OF JAMES

———⬭⬭⬭———

My parents and I finally arrived to the house of Levi. "Dinah, the house of James is here." Her father yelled upstairs.

While our parents were welcoming one another I peeped Dinah looking down the stairs over the balcony, once she noticed me looking at her, she ran back into her room in a frenzy. Five minutes later she came down the stairs with a total different look. She gave me a friendly hug before going into the kitchen to greet my parents.

"Oh my, look it here. Dinah you still look gorgeous as always." My mother said.

"Aint she. Man these kids are really growing up on us." My dad agreed.

"You know I want you to be my future daughter in law." My mom went on. Here they go with that again.

"Tamar and I was just talking about that earlier." I heard her dad say. I don't have no problem with it, but me and Dinah has a lot of catching up to do.

When she re-entered the living room, she grabbed the remote and flipped through the channels until she saw some cooking show on the screen. She was acting like I wasn't sitting on the other couch. Her eyes were glued all in that show. I heard laughter and good vibes coming from our parent's way. I guess I'm gonna have to break the silence.

"So, where Simeon at?" I asked.

"This is usually around the time he gets off work, he should be in shortly." She responded while her eyes still hooked on the TV. I guess that didn't help. I'll try back in a few minutes. Only if she could give me the same attention as she was giving this show and we would be good. She was really sitting on the other couch ignoring my presence.

"Dinah." I whispered. She gave me a slight look before looking at the tv once again.

"Dinah." I whispered again, only with a different tone of voice. I guess that got her attention.

"Yes, Jeremiah." She replied in an irritated tone.

"You just gonna sit over there on the couch and shut me out like that."

"Jeremiah aint nobody shutting you out, conversation goes both ways."

"Attitude."

"Naw, I don't have no attitude."

"Well, if you don't have an attitude, talk to me. Let's go for a walk and feel the night breeze."

"A walk?"

"Yeah, when I was driving over here. I saw a river walk about three to five minutes away."

"You know that's not up to me. You have to ask my dad."

"You saying that like it's hard to do."

"I'm just saying, when he look at you crazy and you get rejected, don't be upset."

"Your dad loves me." I said as I got up and made my way towards the kitchen.

"Excuse me. I'm sorry to interrupt y'alls laughter and everything, but Mr. Levi, I was wondering if Dinah and I can go for a walk?"

"A walk, where?" Levi said as he took a sip of his beer.

"I saw a river walk up the street, were just trying to do some catching up."

"Yeah, y'all can go. If it's okay with your parents and remember don't do nothing to knock points from your good name, you hear me and bring her back in an hour. I'm trying to trust you."

"You got it, Mr. Levi. Whatever you say is what applies."

"Alright, now son, y'all gon' head and like Levi said you bring his daughter back in here an hour later untouched, if you know what I mean. Do you hear me?"

"Yes dad I hear you. Understood."

"James, you know that's what I meant, but I couldn't find a way to put it in a friendlier way." Levi and my dad laughed while I was walking back into the living room.

"They said yeah."

"Is that so? Hmm. My dad is showing me a different side of him with all this. But let me get my jacket."

"Well, I have that effect on people."

"Don't get puffed up." She rolled her eyes as she put on her blue Adidas jacket.

Chapter Thirty-One

PRINCE CHARMING

We were really together, not like that, but I mean in each other's presence and although I wanted to deny it, it felt good.

"So, what's been up with you, Dinah? It's been about six years." Jeremiah said as he wrapped his arm around my shoulder.

"Yeah, I guess."

"You still look good."

"I might look like I've been doing pretty good, but it hasn't been all good with me."

"What do you mean? Talk to me."

"I got into some trouble last year."

"Dinah, in trouble. Nahh."

"Jeremiah, I'm serious and as much as I can't stand talking about it, I feel like you have the right to know."

"Damn, this must really be serious, huh." He turned towards me.

"Yeah, so, I, um. I, um." My eyes whaled with tears. Damn, I could never hold my tears in when talking about this. "I was held against my will and forced into escorting last year." I sniffled.

"Are you serious." He said as he put his head down in disbelief. "Damn, man this shit is unreal." He cuffed his fist and shook his head. The look on his face read "Who did this, so I can get at them." It was like he wanted to fight the air.

"The guy who held me against my will and forced me into that business is in jail."

"That's not enough. Somebody had you out on the streets working for them, pimping you out." He stood up walking back and forth shaking his head. "I hope he didn't make you…"

Already knowing what he was talking about I responded. "No, thank god, but the things he made me do was degrading enough."

"Man, you telling me this, just got me all out the spirit, but it's not about me right now. I wanna know what toll that took on you."

"I mean how you want me to feel. He degraded me, made me feel low. He forced me into that lifestyle and because of that, I feel like I lost a piece of my dignity, lost a piece of myself, my self-esteem, my thought process. I didn't reach my goal of graduating on time. It was all bad, and to me it still is."

"Dinah, look at me. Don't talk like that. I can help you get through this. I care about you and if somebody hurt you, that mean they hurt me. I'm not gonna act like it's all good, because it's not. I can't believe somebody had my future wife out there life that."

Did he just say future wife?

"I take responsibility on my part." Jeremiah grabbed my hands. I was in Cali and I didn't keep in touch. I feel like I was being selfish and only thinking about myself."

"Jeremiah, really it's not your fault."

"No, I blame myself, because if I would have kept in touch, you probably wouldn't have had to go through what you went through. Who is this low-down clown, who forced you?"

"It was some big-time drug dealer from Glenview, who claimed my brother owed him some money and took me into that business as payback. He got twenty-five years in prison and I got a 20,000-dollar settlement, but that comes with its wins and losses."

"What do you mean?" Jeremiah replied trying to process all that I was telling him

"I mean every time I put my house key in the door to the

beautiful brick home we live in, I'm reminded of what I had to go through. Every time I get in my car, flashbacks appear in my head. Every time I go shopping, I'm reminded of that lifestyle. I feel like we're living off my pain and suffering. So, if you look at me differently now, I'll understand."

"Dinah, don't talk like that. It's not your fault. I wanna help you. I want to boost your self-esteem back up. I want to be the person you think about to overshadow your past. I want you to feel protected when you're in my presence. I wanna court you. I wanna prove you. You're the one I seek to become one with."

When he said that, I was speechless. He said it with so much passion. I knew his words were genuine. Little did he know, his motivation had me already feeling a little better. We hugged each other as tears began to slightly fall from my face. It was tears of joy. He really had my back, to the point where I could feel the feeling he had for me. Jeremiah and I being on the level we both always wanted since we were youngins was finally coming into fruition.

"Thank you."

"You're welcome. Now, let me get you back in the house. Your father said I only had one hour with you and I would hate to get on his bad side, especially not while they're in there drinking."

I laughed while wiping my eyes and getting up from the

bench. We made our way back towards the house, where we finished our conversation.

"I'm serious about what I said, Dinah. I don't see nobody else in my future."

"I don't know, I mean, you didn't call or check up on me in six years." I joked.

"I acknowledged that I didn't and apologized. You holding grudges now?" He joked back.

"I'm just saying. I don't know what you were getting into, in Cali."

"You gonna pull that card, you wrong for that one." He laughed.

"I'm just messing with you. Let me think on it and of course you have to run it by my father and then we'll go from there.

"Will do."

"We'll see." I responded as I open the living room door.

"Were back." Jeremiah said loud enough so that our parents could hear in the kitchen.

"Both of y'all come here." I heard my dad say. We walked in the kitchen and presented ourselves.

"Did y'all have fun by the Riverwalk?"

"Yeah, we just did some catching up, like I intended." Jeremiah answered.

"Y'all know y'all wasn't alone." My dad stated. We both

looked at each other and then gave him a confused look. "I told you I got eyes everywhere."

I knew that security guard, who check ID's for the Riverwalk looked familiar.

"Six years' worth of catching up in less than one hour, you good boy." Said James.

"Just the latest, that's all." I replied.

"Well y'all better gon' get y'all some food." My mother added.

"Mr. Levi can I speak with you before the night is out."

Oh my gosh, don't tell me he's gonna run it by my father that fast. I guess he's really staying true to his word. The zeal was real. I thought while making our plates.

"Yeah, I got you, talk to me after you eat."

***

"So, you wanna talk business, huh?" Levi said as he pulled Jeremiah to the side while things were winding down.

"Yes, sir. I was gonna ask for your approval to court Dinah."

"You wanna prove my baby girl, huh? So, what's your plans for her?"

"I want to court for some time, make sure we both graduate, start looking for a house and when the time is right, lord's will, I'll be asking you for your blessing to take her hand in marriage."

"You know you one sharp brother, I like that in you. You not just telling me what I wanna here, are you?"

"No, sir. I wouldn't do that to you or your wife."

"Good, you better not or it will be problems." Levi paused for a while, making sure he prepared what to say. "Okay, you have my approval to court Dinah, but with stipulations, so you might wanna write this in your notes."

Jeremiah, showing that he was serious, took out his phone and accessed his quick memo app. "I'm listening, sir."

"Okay, you are to check in with me every other week. You are to keep a job. You are to let me know when y'all are looking to go out to eat, to the movies or hang out, so that I can make sure I have eyes present. Also, I don't mind you coming over, but no bedroom; open areas only. Also, I know I'm not your father, but you two are to stay on top of your studies. My daughter can't be marrying no dumb brother and you can't be marrying no simple sister, you hear?"

"Yes, sir. Understood on all things."

"Good, gone head now, I gotta speak with your father, may you and my daughter have a happy proving process." Once Levi spoke with Jeremiah and laid the hammer down on what he expected from him. Jeremiah went into their bathroom. He looked himself in the mirror, to examine himself knowing he wasn't the man Levi wanted him to be, yet.

It was a lot expected out of him. Feeling engulfed in anxiety he threw cold water on his face and took a deep breath, processing it all. He was about to approach Dinah; who had no clue of the conversation Jeremiah just had with her father. He put on his "Everything's good face" before walking into the living room.

"So, what happened?" She asked as he sat on the couch next to her.

"Oh, yeah, he approves of us courting, but I'll tell you one thing; it wasn't easy."

"That's my daddy for you." She shook her head while smiling at the same time.

"So, I guess this is the part, where we exchange numbers."

"Yeah, I guess so." The awkwardness was real. Both, Jeremiah and Dinah didn't know how to feel. It was a weird, but happy feeling at the same time.

After Jeremiah stored Dinah's number in under "Future Wife" he turned to her and said. "I'm glad we made it to the next level. Can't see what's in store for us.

Chapter Thirty-Two

PHYSICAL THERAPY

Xavier was spending his second day in Lakeview's Physical Therapy and Rehabilitation center. The nurses have started doing leg strengthening activities with him as well as leg rotation exercises. He was happy that in about a week or so, he'll be back on his feet like he never left.

Although his leg exercises were coming along, two days without talking to Dinah had him in a mild frenzy. His phone went dead a few hours after arriving at Lakeview. That's where he realized he had left his charger behind at Hope Valley Hospital. He couldn't text, call, get on Facebook, Instagram, nothing. He was out of the loop for two whole days.

"Damn, man. I need a charger." He said to himself.

"How are you doing Mr. Wells." One of the nurses asked.

"I'm doing alright."

"How about that leg?"

"It's actually feeling a lot better, thanks to those leg activities and exercises."

"That's awesome, that's what Lakeview is all about making sure our patients are in good care. Did you want me to take you to the dayroom? They have games, a pool, snacks, and much more."

"I'm good in here for now, thank you though."

"No problem, later, I'm gonna bring you the menu for tonight. You get to choose between fried chicken, broccoli and a baked potato or Chicken alfredo with breadsticks."

Sounds good, do you happen to have an iPhone charger."

"As a matter of fact, I do. Let me do my rounds first and then I'll bring it to you."

"Thanks so much. That just made my day."

"You kids and this technology." Nurse Karen laughed. "I'll have it to you in about thirty minutes."

Thirty minutes had passed. Nurse Karen kept her word and put Xavier's phone on charger and made sure it was in arms reach for him. Xavier watched a few tv shows and waited for his phone to charge. At about fifty percent, he was powering on. Once everything loaded up. Notification from apps, texts, calls from the guys and from Dinah was coming through.

He checked a few things, but he couldn't wait to talk to

Dinah. He figured he'll check her message first and go from there.

Clicks on Dinah's Text: *Hey Xavier. Hope Physical Therapy is going good for you. I'm not gonna be able to see you anymore. My dad doesn't approve of our friendship. He told me that as long as I'm under his roof that rule applies. Sorry I have to break this to you. If I'm in the city and I just so happen to see you around, we can speak and be causal. But as far as spending time, I won't be able too. Hope you're not upset.... Best Regards.*

Xavier had to read the text message twice. "Man, hell nawl. I'm not trying to hear none of that." He said aloud. He tried calling, but she didn't pick up. He texted her saying "Can we talk," but he got no reply.

He was livid, but he told himself that he wasn't going to stress it. He know Dinah had been through a lot and probably was just in his feelings. He kept himself busy by watching tv and checking his social media notifications, but the words from Dinah's text kept lingering in his head.

Xavier called his buddy Cruze to get his mind off the situation.

"What's good bro, how they been treating you in there."

"It's been all good, just got back on board, you know my phone been dead for two days."

"I knew it had to be something like that, cuz' I'm like bro always pick up."

169

"Yep, left my damn charger at Hope Valley."

"Damn, but look Uncle Kohl gave me a good lead on the mogs who did this to you."

"I'm listening, what you trying to do, can't have you going back to jail, bro."

"It's still in the works, me and the guys trying to play it smart. Unc was able to get a small clip of video footage from this whole in the wall joint that's right across from that gas station over there. He was able to get me an address that he linked to the license plate number."

"Cruze, I don't know, man. That might be somebody mama's house."

"X, I'm just trying to show mogs. Aint nobody 'bout to come in the View on bull and get away with it."

"Alright bro, I know we gotta prove a point."

"Shit, if it is somebody's mama house, they better lead us to the mogs who did it. They guys who Unc think did it names are Terry and Jamal; the address is 8254 west Dawson."

"That's over there by the Cedar Court Projects."

"Right which leads me to believe, that somebody on the inside was behind it."

"I'm telling you, Tim ass was mad when I went up there and corrected him."

"So, he probably made a deal with some guys in there in

exchange for commissary and supplies. They can't get over on me I was just on the inside."

"Right, y'all got it. Handle that. I'll get back at you later, bro."

"Likewise, get that leg to moving, so we can be back on the move."

"You a fool, bye."

When Xavier got off the phone with Cruze a message from Dinah appeared.

Dinah's Text: Xavier, I have to move forward. I can't be getting caught up. I'm sorry this is what it has come to, but it has come, and just head's up; ya boys could be getting themselves into serious trouble, via word of mouth. Again, my apologies, if I lead you to think something else of us. Good Bye, Xavier.

"She cannot be serious right now. You not about to come here and play on my emotions that I rarely show, and barley got. Shutting me out like I'm some damn fool." Xavier thought to himself.

Xavier's Text: So that's it. Forget about the visits, the tutoring, the talks, the laughs, the gifts. That just don't matter, huh.

While texting her, a message from Tiffany popped up.

Tiffany's Text: Hey, Xavier. I'm sorry about what I said. I hope you can forgive me. I shouldn't have never came to Hope Valley causing a scene like that. It's a time and place for everything and that wasn't the right time nor place.

"Here I was trying to do right to prove myself to Dinah, when It was a girl begging for me to show her some attention. I guess Dinah's ass really isn't worth the trouble." Xavier thought to himself.

Xavier's Text: Apology accepted.

Tiffany couldn't believe what she was reading. For a second, she thought Xavier was really playing games with her.

Tiffany's Text: Really, you really mean it. Thank you, but I gotta ask. What's gotten into you?

Xavier's Text: Girl, you know you ask too many questions. Meet me at Lakeview Rehab center and bring me something good to eat.

After texting Tiffany, something told him to search Dinah's name on Facebook. Something that he never thought of doing, being that he thought they were on a personal level.

He went to her Facebook page to see if anything had changed with her. Xavier scrolled down her page where he saw a few statuses of influential quotes and excitement of possibly being on the dean's list for her honor roll status and high college G.P.A. That was all fine and dandy, but there it was. It was where someone on Facebook named @Prince-Jeremiah who tagged Dinah in a status. This is how Xavier viewed it.

Prince Jeremiah

We do things the right way over here. Glad I finally got her father's approval. When I truly want something, I go for it. @DinahIsrael. #6YearsInTheMaking #CourtingChronicles.

"That's what it is, huh." Xavier said to himself. After doing a little lurking on Jeremiah's page, he got more clarification as to what was going on.

"So, this guy moves from Cali, to the suburbs of Glenview, get back in Dinah's family graces and just like that, they're a thing... X, stop tripping off her ass, didn't you say she wasn't worth it." He said aloud to himself.

Chapter Thirty-Three

TIFFANY IS BACK

"I told you my advice will work girl. Trust your best friend." Adrienne went on after Xavier accepted my apology. "Guys love genuine apologies, what he say after he said apology accepted?" She asked.

"He told me where he was located and asked me to bring him some food."

"Hold em up, Tiff. Why can't "Miss Prissy." bring him some food? Seem like trouble in his court."

"Adrienne, I don't care about that or her." I said as I flipped my 16 inch Brazilian wavy.

"I'm just saying Tiffany, I don't wanna see you getting caught up again."

"Best friend I feel you, but I've been wanting X to accept my apology for three years now and I'm finally getting it. I'm not just about to turn that down. So, with that being said, can I borrow your car?"

"You get on my nerves, Tiff. You better be lucky I feel like binge watching on Netflix. You got three and a half hours with my car and make sure you put some gas in it."

"Okay, okay. Thank you so much Adrienne." I gave her a big hug.

"Girl, get off me and where do you think you going like that, you gotta go in there surpassing what ole girl came thru with. C'mon, let's pick something from my closet."

Adrienne swung open her closet door that was filled with clothes, shoes, heels, purses, cute hats, and jewelry.

"While, I'm thinking of a master piece, go in the bathroom and plug up those curling irons. Weave got be on point, curls gotta be tight.

My best friend was treating this like a red-carpet event, but I wasn't gonna stop her. She laid two outfits on her bed and told me to choose. I fell in love with her shimmery off the shoulder top and her blue and gold maxi skirt. I put it on and once she curled my weave real quick I was out the door. I was gonna stop at Miss Shirley's soul food and cuisine to get X some food like he asked, and I was gonna be on my way.

***

"Hello I'm here for Xavier Wells." I said as I walked up

to the front desk of the Rehab center.

"Can I see your ID, and can you sign in for me." The receptionist asked.

After I signed in, the receptionist gave me visitors pass with my name on it. "Xavier Wells is in room 314, walk straight and the elevator will be to your right."

"Thank you." I rode the elevator with a smile on my face, trying to hold it in. I started walking slow as I walked thru the hallway of the third floor looking for the room number. I had approached 310, so I know I was getting closer. I rubbed my lips together, ran my hand through my hair and continued walking. I had reached 314. I saw X before he saw me. He was just sitting there with a serious look on his face watching tv. "Okay let's see where this goes." I whispered to myself.

"Knock, Knock." I got his attention.

"Hey, you got here kinda fast."

"Sounded like somebody I care about was in need, so I didn't slack."

"Is that right?" He asked. His voice made that question sound so good.

"Yeah, so I brought you some perch, spaghetti, greens and peach cobbler."

"Don't tell me you went to Miss Shirley's."

"You already know."

"Man, her food be so damn good, I aint had her in about three years."

"That's because you aint been around me in three years, I use to make sure you was straight."

"I can't even front, you did. Where you going looking all dressed up anyways?"

"Coming to see you."

"So, you want me to believe that you got dressed up to come down to a rehab center to see me." He said while breaking a piece of his fish.

"Ugh, yeah. Why is that so hard to believe."

"I'm glad you came for real, though."

I leaned back in my seat in awe, he was being a little bit too nice. "Okay, Xavier, what's going on. You scaring me." I giggled, but was very serious.

"Nothing, it just took me some time to realize that, I got somebody that's down for me, right in my face." He replied. What he said made me feel like we had hope.

"That's what I've been trying to show you for the longest, X. Like, when I found out what happened to you, I was mad I didn't find out sooner. I knew what transpired three years ago was going to get in the way, but I figured it was worth a shot."

"I feel you."

"Speaking of three years ago. I wanna show you that

I'm innocent. Your homeboy Rodney's cousin made up a lie about me. He was trying to come at me and when I set him straight in front of his guys, he went back telling Rodney and the rest of his homeboys that I tried something with him and I was writing him anonymous letters in jail. Honestly, I don't even know that boy real name."

"Damn, Tiff, I feel slow. I never did hear your whole side of the story, but it was like he was coming back with letters and everything trying to state his claim."

"Well, they wasn't from me, but I mean I do understand. You didn't want to look like you were being played in front of your guys, plus that was around the time you and your mom was going through y'all little problems."

"Yeah, I'm sorry, Tiff." He reached and grabbed my hand. Oh my gosh, my dream is coming true."

"How's mama Norah doing any ways?"

"She's in rehab. She came up to see me once. She look like she's been doing really well. Three months clean so far, hopefully she can keep fighting the fight."

"That's good, I'm proud of her. So, when you get out of here, where you're gonna be staying at."

"I'm going back to the house."

3342 south Parkway, oh how I remember that house. Me and X went through a lot there. When his mom was short on some bills or wasn't able to pay, I came through. I made sure their light bill was paid, I made sure their refrigerator was stocked. I was there when Xavier needed a shoulder to lean on in the middle of the night. Not that girl or anybody else, it was me.

"So, who was that girl, I saw come up to Hope Valley for you?" I asked.

"What girl?"

"C'mon now, X. You know what I'm talking about."

"Aww, that girl. She was just a girl who was helping me out with tutoring."

"Tutoring?"

"Yeah, you know I was going back to school to get my GED."

"Nawl, I didn't know that, but it looked like you treated her more than just a tutor."

"Yeah, was trying to fill that void."

"Bad boys need love too, huh."

"You crazy, Tiff. I aint out there like that no more."

"Look like she aint from these parts of the tracks."

"Yeah and nawl, but like I said, you gotta ride with who you struggled with."

Whoever ticked X off, thank you, because he's finally coming to his senses. "Well, I'm gonna get out of here, gotta make a few more runs before I gotta give Adrienne back her car. She got me on a three-and-a-half-hour time limit on her car."

"Aww, okay. You know I should be getting out of here by next week, hit me up, maybe you can swing by."

"Okay, I can take you up on the offer."

"Come here, before you go." He signaled his hands. When I got to the side of the bed. He gave me a kiss on my forehead. I stood there for ten seconds trying to replay the moment.

"Okay, call me, X." I said before leaving out of the room. As soon as I got in the car. I called Adrienne

"Best Friend."

"Somebody sounds happy."

"Girl, the visit went better than expected."

"Really, what happened?

"We talked, he was being nice, we nipped that situation from three years ago in the bud."

"Oh wow, Tiff. So, do you think y'all can be how y'all once was?"

"Maybe, he did offer me to come by the house, when he fully recovers."

"What's that all about? Don't go over there playing mommy and wife."

"Shut up, Adrienne. You slow. I'm about to hit the expressway. I'll tell you the rest when I get there."

Chapter Thirty-Four

LOCKED AND LOADED

⎯⎯⎯∞⎯⎯⎯

Cruze and the guys busted through the back door of 8254 west Dawson. The door opened which lead straight to the living room. "Stop what you doing; where in the hell is Jamal and Terry?" Cruze asked fully masked pointing his gun, with his boys' right behind him. He was the ringleader.

"Oh my gosh, please don't hurt me. I don't know where my son is." She said in fear as she curled up on the couch.

"So, if I search this damn house, I'm not gonna find him?"

"No!" Jamal's mother yelled with fear and trembling.

"Well, how about we play house with mommy until he gets here. Rod, take her ass down to the basement." Cruze ordered. Rodney grabbed her by her arm and told her to follow him. Cruze, Kenny, and Jermaine began to wreck the house. "We gonna show mogs, we aint playing."

***

"Aye, y'all hear that?" Brandon asked his buddies and his sister who was sitting on the porch with him. It sounds like somebody arguing and fighting.

'Look, look over there." Brandon sister pointed as she saw a screen door slam across the street. What she saw was Jermaine making sure the front door was locked. He tried to do it as low key as possible.

"Did y'all just see that? Whoever that was had on all black." Brandon sister Sharon noticed.

"Oh, shit. That's Jamal crib."

"What in the hell is going on in there, is somebody robbing the place?" One of his buddies asked.

"I don't know, but his mom car is parked in front. Let me call Jamal, this is not about to end well."

Brandon dialed Jamal. "Yoo."

"Jamal, this is Brandoe. Listen to what I'm about to say. Somebody is in y'all crib. We hear a lot of commotion, like somebody robbing the place.

"Say, what? Terry turn the car around-- Brandoe, you sure it's my crib."

"Yes, me, my sister and solo and them just peeped the whole scene."

"Please, don't tell me my mom car out there man." Jamal said as he balled up his fist and scrunched up his face.

"Bro, it is. Just get here quick. I'll call you if I hear more."

"Bet, be there in five minutes."

"Terry please tell me you got your piece on you." Jamal raged.

"What the hell is going on, man?"

"Brandoe just said he think somebody ran up in the crib while my momma there. On everything, if niggas put my mom's in any harm, it's murder she wrote. No questions asked." When Terry heard that, he began driving faster.

***

"If you don't tell me where Jamal or Terry is, it's gonna be a problem." Cruze stood in front of Jamal's mother.

"Please, what is this about? Do he owe you money? How much it is? I will write you out a check right now." She said weeping while tied up.

"Nah, what Jamal and Terry did is worth more than just money."

Scrrr. You heard the car screeching as it swerved around the corner. That sound had everybody in the neighborhood attention. Jamal and Terry hopped out of the car. At this point people was coming from out of their houses trying to see what was going on.

When Jamal and Terry approached the house, they notice it had been wrecked.

"I hope these niggas didn't take my mom man." Jamal said angered. "Stay right here, bro. My piece is in my shoebox." Jamal went to his room, only to notice when he looked in his shoebox his gun was gone.

"Bro I think these niggas still here. I just heard something; sound like it's coming from the basement." Terry noticed.

***

"Like I said, stop all that damn crying and tell me where Jamal and Terry is at." Cruze demanded.

"Aww, hell nawl. They in my damn house, questioning my mama." Jamal began walking towards the basement.

Terry pulled him back. "Bro, we gotta play this smart."

"Man, hell nawl, that's my mama we talking about. I'll die for mines."

"Look, let's go around the back way to get to the basement. You know that door you use to sneak in and out of in high school that nobody knows is there; let's go through there, that way they won't even hear us coming."

"You not understanding, bro. I'm trying to go in."

"Jamal, listen to me. I been rocking with you since the third grade. I'd be damned if I let anything happen to you or your family."

They tiptoed to the back. "I'm not gonna go in there

with my gun pointed, I wanna catch these niggas off guard." Terry pitched his plan. They both heard the washing machine going. I guess that was to drown out the noise.

Jamal opened the door slowly. "Man, who the hell are y'all?"

"Nawl, who the hell are y'all?" Cruze and Rod pointed their guns. "Let me guess, y'all just the two niggas we want to see. Y'all sending off shots in Glenview, like shit aint gonna get back to us."

"You got the wrong one." Jamal replied.

"Jamal, baby. What are they talking about?" His mother asked.

"You think we wasn't gonna catch y'all." Cruze asked. Terry is quiet, so he can carry out his plan. At this point, he's trying to reach behind his back to get his gun out.

Cruze, Jermaine, Rodney and Kenny are all strapped with their guns under their shirts.

"One of you niggas better start answering me, or I'll make you miss ya mama." Cruze let out an evil laugh. "Now, y'all think we crazy, like we just let shit slide in the View."

Pow, Pow, Pow. Shot fired.

"Noooo." You heard Jamal say.

Prepared to run out, Cruze asked. "Rodney, what the hell you just do that for? That wasn't the plan."

"Cruze, that nigga was too quiet. I saw him trying to

reach for his piece on the slick, so I popped him."

Cruze and the guys still running made their way to the car.

"Mom, stay right here." Jamal demanded. Jamal took Terry's gun and followed. He ran down the porch stairs, aimed at the car firing shots as Cruze pulled off.

Everybody that were on their porch dropped to the ground, scared for their lives. Jamal ran back to the basement, untied his mother and crawled to where Terry was laying at, with blood coming from his mouth. He shook him. "Terry, don't go out on me, man. Stay with me." At this time, his mom is calling the ambulance. Terry with blood pooling from his mouth let out some gibberish, trying to hold on to the rest of the breath he have left.

Five minutes later, the ambulance and police, came rushing to the basement. They retrieved Terry. They put him in the ambulance truck, where they tried to perform the little they could do, but not long after he entered the ambulance truck, one of the EMT's signaled her hands that it was over for him.

Chapter Thirty-Five

FURIOUS

Jeffro had just finished up his call. He returned to his room. He sat down for a couple of minutes trying to play everything off, but moments later his anger got the best of him. He hopped off his bunk, cracked his neck on each side, before speaking.

"Get yo ass up."

"What, nigga?"

"I said get yo ass up." Jeffro approached Tim as he pulled the seat from up under him.

"Nigga, are you crazy? What the hell is wrong with you?" Tim got in his face.

"One of my lil mans is dead and I'm blaming your ass." He rushed him and began choking him until his back hit the wall. "So, you sending niggas from Glenview to my lil guys' mom house." Although Jeffro was strong, Tim had a bit more muscle. He twisted Jeffro's arm and pushed him against the door.

"Don't you ever come for me like that. You was the main one who offered your guys to take on the hit. With you being a big shot and so-called leader of the streets, you already know what could possibly come with that."

"Nigga, you trying to call me slow. I just lost one of my guys, I'm not trying to hear none of that b.s you coming with and since you wanna throw rank in the mix. You were the leader of South Glenview, so if those niggas sent off shots that mean you sent off shots." Jeffro said as he tried to rush Tim again, but Tim tripped him, putting him in the headlock.

"And why you trying to come at me, your other lil guys raped my ole girl. He took advantage of her and didn't pay his part, so that means that's money outta my pockets, those your guys, so that mean you owe me, since you wanna take it there."

"Man, I'm not trying to hear that. My mans is dead. You think I give a damn about a shameless hoe. She knows what she was getting herself into."

They began fighting, both of them using their strength to try to throw the other against the room. At this point, the guards were rushing to their room to break up the fight and take both of them out.

A few guards had Jeffro and another set of guards had Tim. "This aint over." Jeffro warned. "I know where you from, I'll have your guys dropping like flies."

"Yeah okay, you aint the only ruthless nigga, don't act like I don't have connects, boi." Tim warned.

"So, you two knuckleheads wanna send death threats, right in front of our faces, huh? Well, how about a few days thrown in the hole? You know solitary confinement loves company." The head guard warned them.

Chapter Thirty-Six

CHARACTER COLLISION

This is that part; you know when a movie is about to end, it pauses at every character and let you know what their future holds. Well, this is it, let's get into it.

Dinah: Dinah and Jeremiah began proving one another. They are not hasty to rush into anything. They have been spending time with one another and hanging out, with supervision, of course. Levi, Dinah's father has eyes everywhere, especially after what happened last year. While proving Jeremiah, Dinah is finishing her last semester at Dupointe University, so she can walk across that stage knowing that she earned every piece of her bachelor's degree.

Jeremiah: Jeremiah has gotten back in tune with living in Glenview's suburb. He too is finishing his degree at Dupointe University. Jeremiah has been the happiest guy in town, knowing that he came back from California and accomplished his mission of courting Dinah. After she told him what happened to her, thoughts of viewing her in a different way enters his mind, but the love he has for her will never let those thoughts break up what they are trying to become.

Rachel: After Rachel was raped, she stopped dealing with Tim completely, seeing that all he cares about is himself and his money. Detective Kohl and Officer Lonnie had to report that she was arrested and brought in for questioning, which led to her having to appear in court once more. The judge showed some sympathy being that she was raped this time around. Instead of throwing her back in jail, the judge ordered her to spend eight months in a facility for troubled young women where curfew is limited and strict rules apply.

Xavier: Xavier legs are stronger than ever. Lakeview has really helped him regain the strength he needs. He's back at home. After being shot, some would think he would get out of the game. Nawl, Nawl. He already told y'all in part one that he's been in the streets since he was ten. To him, that's not an easy task to just give up. He did talk a good game about how he wanted to change and get out of that lifestyle, but he ate those words right back up after Dinah didn't want nothing to do with him anymore. Actually, it made him even more uptight and aggressive than before. He and the guys has still been on their same ole mission and that's hustling and getting money.

Tiffany: Tiffany and Xavier have been hanging out.

They both have put their past behind them. She's been at the house with him from time to time doing exactly what her friend Adrienne said she shouldn't do and that's cooking, cleaning and making sure he's good. Tiffany know what Xavier is about, she was with him when he really was in his prime and now that he's back at it, she has no problem with supporting him and his lifestyle as long as he throws her a couple hundreds to maintain her.

Desire: Desire is still in college and living by her father's rules. She recently got a job, so she can show her father that she can be responsible and help out around the house, being that her mother left them because she didn't want to hearken to her husband's views and rules.

Tim: Tim is still doing his 25-year bid. After getting placed in the hole for a few days for fighting Jeffro, he came to his senses on how he treated Rachel, but that doesn't mean his money-making business ends, you won't believe who he has working for him now. Jeffro and Tim never said the real reason why they were fighting; they both put their heads together and knew that if one of them said anything about their doings on the outside that it would result to added time on their sentence. Someone above all on the inside is going to come offering Tim a sweet deal, that could possibly cut his time in more than half, but it will come with a catch. Tim may be out sooner than you think.

Cruze: Cruze has been laying low since they invaded Jamal's mother house. When Rodney shot Terry, he killed him. Rodney fled to the other side of town to avoid getting caught. When that case came up, Cruze uncle, Detective Kohl investigation unit took it over, which kept Cruze and the guys in the clear.

Aunt Shayna: Aunt Shayna felt bad once she found out Rachel was raped. She couldn't let that sit on her mind knowing that she knew what Rachel was doing when she would leave all those nights. She told her husband Uncle Tony how she knew about what was going on, but didn't say nothing, because she knew what she had been through. Uncle Tony wasn't trying to hear none of that, he left the house, because in his mind it's Shayna's fault for what happened to his niece. At the moment, he has no plans of returning home.

Detective Kohl: Detective Kohl has been working on the Terry Hopkins case, in which his nephew Cruze played a part. Kohl has been making sure his name stays in the clear as well as his nephew. He's also been digging deeper into the case and what he found out was all this steamed from Xavier checking Tim over his high school's buddy daughter, Dinah, but what he's trying to figure out is; why didn't Levi say anything when he slightly expressed what was going on at the bar. Things just got real and it may be time for Detective Kohl to pay Levi a visit.

Levi: Levi has been the head of his house as usual. He hasn't been so strict on Dinah, because he knows she is with someone he approves of. If anybody come calling him asking or looking for his daughter, he will do everything in his power to protect her. He has had to reach out to some of his old connections, as his eyes to make sure Dinah is safe, especially when she goes back and forth to the city. His old connections respect him, being that he use to run the Southside, back then before he had kids. When people come questioning him about what part his daughter played in this whole Glenview drama ordeal, he will make it his business to keep her outta harm's way. Will Simeon and Levi have to go on another rampage?

CAST YOUR VOTE!

The sequel to this series depends on you. Who story will you like to read about next? Let us know by casting your vote. Email us at Goldenpennpresents@gmail.com with your name and the next title you would like to read. Let the story with the most votes win.

If All Else Fails: Jeremiah and Dinah's Story.

Becoming Rachel: Take a Walk in My Shoes.

Cold World: The Story of Xavier.

A Girl Named Desire.

They Can't Hold Me Back: The Rise, Fall and Release of Tim.

DISCUSSION QUESTIONS

⎯⎯⎯∞⎯⎯⎯

Answer the discussion questions for your chance to win a Golden Penn prize package. Send your responses to Goldenpennpresents@gmail.com

1. Do you think Dinah uses her beauty and intelligence as a shield to hide insecurities?

2. Do you believe Dinah's father is too hard on her, being that she is 21 years old now? Why or why not?

3. Was Dinah being simple, when she agreed to tutor Xavier? Considering that, he had a close connection to Tim.

4. Do you think Jeremiah charmed his way into Dinah and her family lives or do you believe that it was truly meant to be?

5. By, Tim ordering a hit out on Xavier; and Dinah coming to his aid, which affects her emotionally. Is it safe to say, Tim still wields influences on her life, even from behind bars?

6. Do you think Dinah's father courting stipulations was a bit too much? Why or why not?

7. Was Rachel rape, what she deserved, being that she has been living a risky lifestyle?

8. Did Xavier connect with Tiffany genuinely or is he only getting in touch with her because Dinah dismissed him?

9. Do you think Detective Kohl is a crooked cop? Was he in the wrong for helping his nephew?

Made in the USA
Monee, IL
21 July 2020